Dear Reader,

I've been sentenced to hard labor, in the first salaried position of my privileged life. But when my father threw out the challenge—to hold a job for thirty days without invoking the family name or fortune—I couldn't refuse. After all, it wasn't the family honor at stake, but my own. Not to mention a 1932 Silver Shadow.

This is how I find myself driving a truck and toting a piano throughout the state of Nevada. I wouldn't be able to take the boredom if I didn't have the mystery of an elusive employer.

From "Chopsticks" to Tchaikovsky, my new boss is a master of classical music. But for some reason, she's hiding her talent in barrooms in backwater towns. I've been known to have a way with women, and before the month is over, I intend to have her spilling her secrets, or my name's not...

Antony Graham Wellington IV

Nevada

MEN
MADE IN AMERICA

BARBARA BRETTON
Nobody's Baby

Nevada

HA #230

Harlequin Books

TORONTO • NEW YORK • LONDON
AMSTERDAM • PARIS • SYDNEY • HAMBURG
STOCKHOLM • ATHENS • TOKYO • MILAN
MADRID • WARSAW • BUDAPEST • AUCKLAND

For Big Mel—Wally's #1 pal—with *much* love.
Thanks, Pop.
and
For Connie Flannery, treasurer of the
Mr. Ed's-Not-Dead Fund. You couldn't be 201?

 HARLEQUIN ENTERPRISES LTD.
225 Duncan Mill Road, Don Mills,
Ontario, Canada M3B 3K9

NOBODY'S BABY

ISBN: 0-373-45178-4

Published Harlequin Enterprises, Ltd. 1988, 1993

Printed in the U.S.A.

Prologue

Hank Wiley hadn't made his millions by being a fool, and if his granddaughter, Jill, thought she could trick him the way she tricked his idiotic daughter and his tennis-playing son-in-law, the girl was dead wrong.

Jill didn't smile one damn *real* smile from the minute they sat down at the dinner table until she headed into the ballroom to play piano for the Palm Beach Women's Guild.

She fiddled with her pale blond hair and fussed with the collar of her bright yellow dress and fumbled around with the collection of knives and forks and spoons that seemed to multiply on the table faster than jackrabbits in heat, but she had never really smiled.

Oh, she ate and drank and talked with the best of them, but Hank Wiley's eyes were still sharp, and he wasn't fooled. Jill, child of his heart, delight of his soul, was unhappy and that was something he couldn't abide.

The only time she looked happy was sitting at that big grand piano of hers, and she didn't sit at that piano often enough to suit him.

It didn't take a genius to see she was hurting and hurting bad. Her huge gray eyes usually flashed with fire and life, but there wasn't so much as a spark when she looked at Tyler Austin.

The slug.

Hank narrowed his eyes and stared at the handsome, strapping young man sitting in the back row. He supposed there was really nothing wrong with the boy except the fact that his family had been inbreeding so long his blood probably ran bluer than the sky over old Palm Beach.

But, then, there'd been nothing obviously wrong with her ex-husband either, and see where that ended up. His philandering had cost Jill that baby she'd wanted so bad, and when it looked like no other little Wyatts were going to make an appearance, that low-life bastard had crawled on his craven belly to his divorce lawyers and let them break the news.

Money was great—Hank would be the first one to admit that—but money didn't cushion all the blows life threw at you.

And money couldn't buy Jill the one thing she needed: a man, a real man, a man who gave as good as he got and would be her partner through the highs and the lows.

The kind of man Hank had in mind didn't flourish beneath palm trees or on fancy yachts. He looked over at her as she played her longhair music for a group of old peahens who were just looking for an excuse to get together and chew the fat.

She finished one selection, and he watched as Tyler applauded politely.

The kind of man Hank had in mind would never wear a pink handkerchief no matter how many highfalutin designers said it was the latest thing.

Hell, the kind of man Hank had in mind probably didn't even exist but, if he did, she sure didn't stand a chance of finding him so long as she was east of the Mississippi.

She needed a man like the men he'd grown up with. A man like the men he'd patterned his own self after.

A man only the American West could grow.

Tyler Austin caught Hank looking at him and smiled politely. *No,* Hank thought. *You ain't the one for Jill.*

For far too long, her eyes had held a look of sadness that nothing seemed able to wipe away. And now she was about to give into loneliness and propriety and his damned daughter's infernal pressure and slide head-first into another marriage bound to break her heart— and maybe even her spirit this time, as well.

Hank lit another cigar and ignored his son-in-law's polite cough. If the man was too well-bred to say "Put out that stinkin' stogie, old man," then he deserved whatever he got.

It was Jill he was worried about.

Back before she married, Jilly had dreams of a career in music. Big, Technicolor dreams of traveling the country, of excitement and glamour and the happiness that came with doing what she was meant to do.

"Money's no object," she used to say, making Hank laugh at the statement only a rich kid could say with such conviction. "I'll play anywhere, for anybody who'll listen. All I want to do is make music."

Well, where was that fire? Gone, that was where. Her marriage had dampened the spark, and her divorce had extinguished the fire.

Two of the old battle-axes near the French doors to his left were whispering, their pale blue cotton-candy heads pressed close together.

"They say she hasn't gotten over losing the baby," one said. "They say—"

"Damnation," Hank muttered, storming out of the room.

It was high time someone reminded her that she was a Wiley and Wileys never gave up. There was a whole world out there filled with people who'd like to hear her play her piano. Maybe they weren't in Palm Beach, or cozied up in Carnegie Hall but they were real people with real needs and real emotions, and maybe one of them would be the real man she deserved to find.

Hellfire.

He was going to break Jill loose or know the reason why.

Chapter One

MANHATTAN
Two weeks later

What's wrong with this picture?

Antony Graham Wellington IV leaned back in his leather chair and looked at the four aristocrats seated around the table playing draw poker that Tuesday afternoon in mid-March.

Parker Sloane-Thompson of the London Thompsons held two kings.

Edward Wheeling Brewer of the Chicago Wheelings and the Delaware Brewers held the two, three and four of diamonds and very little hope.

Maxwell Taylor Brody, of mysterious origins and overwhelming wealth, held three jacks and a queen.

And his father, Antony Graham Wellington III, held a handful of hearts and the knowledge that he was going to wipe up the floor with his old cronies.

The men delighted in ways to cheat one another, from sticking extra aces under the brandy decanter to hiding poker chips in the pockets of their Hardy Amies suits when, in truth, they had but to look at the reflections in the others' sturdily upper-class bifocals to know exactly what each man held.

That, of course, would take all the fun out of it.

And then there was Tony, son and heir to all the worldly goods accumulated by Antony Graham Wellington, Antony Graham Wellington, Jr., Antony Graham Wellington III and a list of Wellingtons and Grahams and Parkhursts—on his late mother's side—who had worked hard and invested wisely so Tony could lose ten thousand dollars during an afternoon card game.

Two hundred years of superior breeding and it all came down to an inside straight.

As usual, it was driving Tony crazy.

Rafaela had flown off to her assignment in Hawaii the day before yesterday and, instead of feeling depressed, he felt relieved. She'd begun to look around the corners of their relationship and muse on the possibility of a future with him, and the future was one thing that interested Tony not at all.

Good-time Tony. Love 'em and leave 'em. Hell, love 'em and don't leave 'em. Make them smile. Make them laugh. Keep things light and breezy and safe, but keep moving before you have a chance to make promises you sure as hell weren't going to remember in the morning.

He was never cruel, never anything but honest about the fact that what there was, was all there would ever be. The women he was with understood right from the start that when it came to permanence, he was the wrong man.

Not even Yale had been able to teach him any other way, and, in twenty-eight years, no one had ever been able to make him wonder why he'd never tried to learn.

He believed in keeping life simple, his options open and his select lovers as friends for as long as they were willing to play by his rules.

But lately he'd been feeling something he didn't quite understand, a loneliness as foreign to him as the Latin writing on the plaque over the front door of the venerable old Emory Club.

For a split second with Rafaela he had considered the possibility of letting their relationship deepen, of exploring all the avenues of emotional involvement open to a man and a woman who liked each other more than a little, but the truth was, Tony Wellington simply didn't know how.

How better to escape these unsettling feelings than with an afternoon of cards and, if he were lucky, a good argument.

He waited while the other men discarded and drew again, then reached for the pot in the center of the table.

"Gentlemen," he said wearily, "youth will have its way."

Mr. Wellington III put his hand over the pile of chips. "Not that I doubt your word, Tony, but let's see your cards."

"My cards? I'm not the one who hides cards in his argyle socks, Father."

Edward Brewer cleared his throat. "I don't hide cards in my socks, Tony. It slipped."

"A jack of clubs just happened to slip into your sock?"

"I say, son," Max Brody broke in, "are you implying Brewer cheats?"

Tony leaned back in his chair and poured himself another generous splash of Napoleon brandy. "You all cheat," he said amiably. "Sometimes I think you enjoy the cheating more than the playing."

"It's not cheating," said his father. "It's creative card playing."

"Cheating," Tony shot back. "You gentlemen spend sixty hours a week trying to think of ways to give away your money, then you come here and cheat like hell to win at poker." He drained his brandy snifter. "It just goes to prove my theory."

Mr. Wellington III groaned and reached for the brandy himself. "Not that blasted theory again." He poured himself two fingers' worth and pushed the decanter toward Sloane-Thompson. "You're becoming a bore."

"And you've become an anachronism."

"Wealth and privilege are the right and proper results of a life well lived," said his father.

Tony snorted into his third brandy. "You sound like a shill for the *Fortune* 500."

Brewer turned to Sloane-Thompson. "There's something wrong with the *Fortune* 500?"

Sloane-Thompson shrugged his shoulders and turned toward Brody who seemed to be enjoying the whole episode.

"This is old territory," Brody said, toasting Tony with his own tumbler of Scotch. "Our young friend is going through the obligatory guilt pangs of one to-the-manor-born. He'll grow out of it."

"Antony has the mistaken notion that the rich are obsolete," Mr. Wellington III elaborated. "Although, I must say we rarely have this discussion when he's driving his Maserati or heading toward Cap d'Antibes."

"Useless," Tony corrected as he snatched the decanter of brandy away from Edward Brewer. "Not obsolete." He should know. No one his age should have so much time to kill.

"Is he a Communist?" Sloane-Thompson asked.

"No," said Mr. Wellington. "He's a radical Democrat." Which to many of the rich meant exactly the same thing.

Brody was still sputtering into his brandy. "Useless? What does he mean by useless?"

"I'm only his father," Mr. Wellington said. "I sired him; that doesn't mean I have to understand him."

Tony was so elated to have an argument to sink his teeth into that he didn't notice the edge to his father's voice.

"I'd be happy to explain the meaning of *useless*." He pointed toward the playing cards and poker chips scattered on the antique mahogany table. "Example number one: Who else but the rich and useless would be playing poker at two-thirty on a Monday afternoon in March?" *With the possible exception of 30 thousand gamblers in Las Vegas...*

Brody poured himself another Scotch while Brewer and Sloane-Thompson mumbled to each other. Mr. Wellington III, however, glared straight at Tony.

"Come on, gentlemen," Tony continued, gathering up the cards then shuffling the deck. "You don't think this is the normal workday of the American male, do you?"

Sloane-Thompson vibrated with righteous indignation. "By whose definition of normal? I say, young man, perhaps you have little regard for your place in society, but I, for one, am proud of my lineage and my role in this world."

This was even better than usual. As a rule, the most he could get out of his father's poker cronies was a mild "Stuff it," followed closely by "Ante up."

Tony executed a perfect waterfall shuffle and started to deal out seven-card stud. "If they dropped the bomb on the Emory right now, no one would even miss us. In fact—"

To Tony's astonishment, Mr. Wellington slammed his fist down on top of the table and sent chips scattering across the Aubusson carpet.

"That's it," the older man said, his voice the perfect echo of his own father's and his father's father. "You have made this little speech once too often, my boy."

Tony grinned and flipped himself an ace high. "The truth cuts too close to the bone, does it, Father? So you finally admit there's more to happiness than polo and poker and penthouses."

"Definitely," said his father, to the obvious amusement of the other men. "In fact, I don't think you should let money stand in the way of your search for a higher form of happiness." He pulled out his cigarette case and slowly lit a Gauloise the way he always did when savoring a dramatic moment.

Far be it from Tony to ruin a dramatic moment. He continued dealing the cards. He was aware, however, of the edge that had crept into his father's perfectly modulated voice and he found a matching anger growing inside him.

Mr. Wellington the elder exhaled, and a plume of smoke curled around his aristocratic face and continued up toward the ceiling. "If you want to feel useful, you can always tear up your American Express card and your little black book and get a job someplace, Antony. You'd leave a few broken hearts behind, but I'm sure they'd all survive.''

The Messrs. Brewer, Brody and Sloane-Thompson murmured amongst themselves.

Tony, however, saw only his father and heard only the challenge.

"You think I couldn't hold down a real job, don't you?"

"One day on a real job and you'll thank God and mutual funds that we're rich."

"I say you're wrong."

Wellington's bushy dark brows rose over the tops of his eyeglasses. "Are you willing to bet on it?"

Tony tossed his cards down on the table. "Name the terms."

"Thirty days," his father shot back. "Thirty days as a—how did you put it?—useful member of society."

Tony's adrenaline started pumping. "Meaning what?"

His father eyed him the way he eyed most radicals and all Democrats. "Meaning you hold a job for thirty working days."

Tony grinned. "No problem." He'd been on the board of the Wellington trucking firm that went under last year. It hadn't exactly been tough sledding.

His father glowered. "A full-time job."

"I'd already assumed that." He let his gaze linger on each of the men sitting at the table. "I'm young and healthy—how tough can it be?"

His father harrumphed and rang for the butler who quickly brought the daily papers from fifteen major cities in the United States.

"Chicago, New York, San Francisco, Phoenix, Las Vegas, Boston...you name the city."

Tony glanced down at the pile of chips in front of him. "Las Vegas." Why not? Maybe he could get a job as a croupier at Caesar's Palace or pit boss at the Desert Inn. Something he would be good at.

Maybe he could even buy the hotel.

His father plucked the Vegas paper from the stack and handed him the classified section. Tony's grin faded. This was getting serious. One minute he'd been having a great time playing poker and moaning about the aristocracy and the next he was looking through the help-wanted ads. If it weren't a question of honor at this point, he would have dealt his father a royal flush and considered them even.

Too late now.

"Name your poison, Antony. I'll bet you that Rolls you've had your eye on that you don't last a month."

"You know that Rolls I've had my eye on is a 1932 Silver Shadow, don't you?"

"That's how sure I am about it."

He could almost feel the silent cheers of his father's pals. But it was the smug smile on his father's face that pushed Tony over the edge.

He shoved the classified section back toward Wellington III. "You pick the job for me." He smiled back at the older man. "That's how sure I am."

His father ran his finger down a center column. "Tony," he said, "I think I've found the perfect job for you."

HELP WANTED: Male, good driving record, strong, used to manual labor. Knowledge of music a plus. Good salary, all expenses. Must be willing to travel.

Five minutes later Antony Graham Wellington IV, single, twenty-eight years old, of strong body and once of strong mind, placed a long-distance phone call to Las Vegas, Nevada.

And he wondered how his father was going to like the Rolls.

LAS VEGAS
Two weeks later

JILLIAN WILEY KATHRYN VON ERON groaned and put her head down on the top of her grandfather's desk. "This is turning into a nightmare," she mumbled into the collection of job applications piled up on the blotter. "Why did I ever let myself get roped into this?"

"Because you know a good idea when you hear one, girl." Hank was stretched out on the worn leather couch across the room. "This is the best damned thing you've ever done."

The craziest, maybe.

It was hard to believe only three weeks had elapsed since Hank first challenged her on the beach at Palm. "Why wait for people to come to you?" he'd said with that wild West shoot-'em-up attitude she'd always loved. "Maybe it's time for you to go to the people."

Paiute Hollow. Silver Spur. Devil's Heart. Tiny little towns with big dreams. Places where the only live entertainment was the postman's daughter who played the recorder.

It wasn't Carnegie Hall but Jill had long since realized that, despite her Juilliard training, Carnegie Hall wasn't about to knock down her door. Not even if the Von Erons donated a new wing to it.

She'd expected to have a few months to get her mother accustomed to the idea of having a vagabond daughter and to assure Tyler Austin she wasn't disappearing into the wilderness of Las Vegas permanently.

However, she'd forgotten that the same intense drive that had helped Hank Wiley parlay his first Texas-crude fortune into an empire that encompassed a fast-food chain as American as its rival's golden arches and a chain of newspapers that covered the country also applied when it came to family.

Before she had a chance to draw a deep breath, he'd arranged an itinerary for her, begun a publicity campaign, found a Bornsdorfer baby grand and leased a small, air-conditioned truck.

Now all they needed was to hire a driver—something they'd been trying to do since Monday.

Hank tossed another application her way. "I kind of liked that last one, girl. Four years trucking experience, prize-winning weight lifter, two kinds of—"

Jillian raised her head high enough to glare at her grandfather. "He had hair in his ears, Pa. I refuse to hire a man who has hair in his ears."

"He had muscles like that Arthur Schwarzenegger—"

"*Arnold* Schwarzenegger, and I don't care if he can bend steel beams with his teeth. I refuse to be seen with a man with hair in his ears."

"Damnation, girl! We ain't lookin' for Miss America." Her grandfather lit a cigar and puffed furiously. "We been interviewin' for three days now, and you got some dadblamed thing to say about every one of 'em."

"So sue me." She grabbed a cookie from the bag of Chips Ahoy in the upper desk drawer. "I happen to be a woman of high standards."

"Those high standards are gettin' on my nerves, Jilly. You're hirin' a truck driver, not a husband, and you're runnin' out of time."

He happened to be right, but Jill chose to ignore that fact.

Obviously annoyed, Hank got up, grabbed the stack of rejected applications out from under her and waved one beneath her nose. "What was wrong with Clarence O'Day?"

"Clarence O'Day... Clarence O'Day... How could I forget?" She sat straight up. "He bit his nails, wore Canoe and thought Tchaikovsky was a Russian dissident."

"Frank Arvoti?"

"Gold chains. A diamond pinky ring in the shape of a horseshoe."

Even Hank agreed with her on that one.

She looked at the lone application in the "Maybe" pile. "What was wrong with the veterinary student from Oxnard? I thought he had real possibilities."

Hank rested his cigar on the giant marble ashtray to the right of the couch. "Possibilities? That guy was so skinny he couldn't lift a pencil without stopping to catch his breath. What good would he be?"

"He knew everything there was to know about Debussy's concertos."

"You lookin' for someone to gab with, or someone to haul a piano, Jilly? You ain't gonna find everything in one package."

She grabbed another cookie. "You're saying brawn and brains are mutually exclusive, Pa? Sounds suspiciously sexist to me."

"Nothin' sexist about it. Just plain common sense. You're lookin' for a piano-moving truck driver, not a rocket scientist."

"Well," she said, brushing cookie crumbs off her fingers and checking her appointment calendar, "we have four more to go. I don't know about you, but I'm starved. The sooner we get this over with, the sooner we can head out for dinner."

"Is this the guy from up Elko way who used to drive an eighteen-wheeler?"

"That's later. This is the one who called from New York last week to make the appointment."

She pressed the intercom buzzer to let Hank's long-suffering secretary, Emily, know they were ready. "I can see it now," she said as she straightened the lapels on her pale yellow linen suit. "He probably has the IQ of an apple and the personality of a toll taker on the Jersey Turnpike." She smoothed down her hair and checked to make sure her earrings were still in place. "Why am I even bothering with this?"

"Bad attitude," Hank said, sitting upright on the couch. "You just got cold feet, that's all. Your ma's harping about you throwin' your life away got under your skin."

Jill laughed. "I'm starving is what it is. If we don't get through these blasted interviews and get some food, I'm afraid I just might—"

She stopped cold.

A man stood in the doorway, watching them. Instantly she took in the beautifully pressed khaki pants, the dark green polo shirt with the tiny Ralph Lauren logo embroidered on the chest, the well-worn deck shoes and the Rolex knockoff on his left wrist. He was about six feet tall, broad-shouldered, chestnut-haired and ridiculously out of place.

"I'm sorry," she said. "This is a private office. Emily should have been at her desk. If you're looking for the editorial offices of Western News Service, they're down on the second floor."

He smiled, and she noticed the strong, even white teeth, the firm jawline, the marvelous angle of shoulder and waist and leg.

Oh, yes, this one was definitely standing in the wrong doorway.

"Emily isn't out there," he said. "She asked me to tell you she doesn't get paid to work without coffee breaks."

From the couch Hank mumbled a curse about unions. "We're waitin' on an interview," he said, eyeing the man warily. "Unless there's something we can help you with, I'm gonna have to ask you to leave."

The younger man didn't seem fazed by Hank's bluntness. Jill's interest was piqued. Most men backed down when Hank Wiley began to throw his weight around.

"You'd ask me to leave without the interview?" the man in the doorway asked. "I've heard of snap decisions before, but don't I deserve a trial by jury?"

Hank's mumbling escalated in volume.

"Look," she said, stepping between her grandfather and this extremely intriguing stranger, "you don't even know what job we're interviewing for. Why don't you—"

He hooked one thumb through a belt loop and leaned against the doorjamb. No man had the right to look so at home in unfamiliar territory. "Male, good driving record, strong, used to manual labor." He stepped into the office and extended his hand toward Jill. "I also like to travel."

Her hand disappeared within his, and she found herself staring up into a pair of gorgeous green eyes that swept over her body with the warmth of the Nevada sun blazing outside.

"You're Tony Graham? The Tony Graham from New York?"

"Afraid so." He turned toward Hank and shook his hand as well. "Ten minutes late and I apologize. Does that count against me?"

"No," said Jill.

"Yes," said her grandfather.

Tony Graham looked from one to the other. "Listen," he said easily, "if there's some kind of problem, maybe we can reschedule."

He didn't bite his nails. He didn't reek of Canoe. He spoke in complete sentences in a voice devoid of identifiable accent. What on earth was he doing applying for a job as a glorified piano mover? She shot her grandfather a quelling look and motioned for Tony Graham to sit down in the chair adjacent to the desk.

"There's no problem at all," she said, daring Hank to contradict her. "We have plenty of time."

Hank grumbled louder than her stomach had during the last interview and lit up another huge Cuban cigar.

"I thought you wanted to go to dinner," Hank said.

"After the interview," she shot back, aware of Tony Graham standing there, absorbing everything. She turned back and picked up his application form. "I see Emily didn't get very much information from you over the phone. Perhaps you can fill me in. Full name?"

He leaned back in the chair, still at ease, while her nerves did a war dance inside her body. "Tony Graham."

"Is that short for Anthony?"

He shook his head. "Just Tony."

"Address?"

The slightest pause, then, "22 Munsey Hollow, Cold Spring Harbor. Long Island."

That explained the Ralph Lauren polo shirt. "Own or rent?"

"Own."

She looked up. Much of her girlhood had been spent visiting friends in the horsey territory of the North Shore of Long Island. If he owned one of those estates she remembered fondly, he had absolutely no business applying for a job as a truck driver.

"You own a house in Cold Spring Harbor?" She put down her pen. "Really, Mr. Graham, if you've been put up to this, I'd—"

Graham didn't flinch. "Am I applying for a job or a bank loan, Ms. . . . ?"

"Wiley." She'd already decided to go under Hank's last name rather than Von Eron, since Von Eron was synonymous with almost-obscene wealth, but there was something about this man that made her feel as if he could see beneath her ruse. Her cheeks reddened in response. "If you have a problem answering these questions, perhaps we should forgo this interview."

He leaned back in his chair. "I own a condo in Cold Spring Harbor. Three bedrooms, two baths."

"I didn't know they had condos in Cold Spring Harbor." What on earth was the matter with her? Why couldn't she leave well enough alone?

"Mine was one of the first."

"A trailblazer, Mr. Graham?"

He grinned. "Always, Ms. Wiley."

"Age?"

"Twenty-eight."

The next blank on the application form was for height and weight but she decided discretion was the better part of valor in this case and filled in "6 feet" and "180."

He was quiet while she scribbled then he leaned forward and turned the application form around.

"One-eighty? After all the iron I've been pumping?" He scratched out the number with the pen lying on the end table and scribbled in another.

Jill snatched the page back and looked at it. "One-seventy?"

"You don't believe it?"

"I didn't say that."

"I'll get on a scale, if you want me to, Ms. Wiley."

Damn his hide. The man was enjoying himself—and at her expense. Maybe Clarence O'Day with the Canoe and the bitten-up fingernails wasn't so bad after all. At least with O'Day there was no doubt about who was doing the hiring.

This Tony Graham had only been in the room five minutes before she'd lost control of the interview.

Jill took a deep breath and called upon twenty-six years of etiquette lessons to see her through. "Last employer?"

"You're looking at him."

She put down her pen. "I beg your pardon?"

"You asked for my last employer?"

She nodded.

"Well, you're looking at him. I owned a small trucking firm that went bust about eight months ago."

She glanced over at Hank who was sitting on the arm of the leather couch, but her grandfather's face was impassive.

Obviously she was in this on her own.

"What kind of trucking firm?" He didn't look the type to haul produce. Actually, he didn't look the type to do anything at all. He had the air of superior breeding and innate uselessness that she was used to finding in men from a more rarefied background than Tony Graham's.

"I'm afraid it's classified."

He looked dead serious but she was sure she saw a twinkle hidden way back there in his eyes.

"A classified trucking firm? Come now, Mr. Graham. You'll have to do better than that."

He did. "It was a top-secret government contract with SAC Headquarters. Any more than that and I'd be risking national security."

This was getting more bizarre by the second. "I'm surprised that a man so well connected would go out of business. Did you cross swords with someone?"

"Only with Congress. Budget cutbacks, environmental considerations..." His voice trailed off. "A small business doesn't stand a chance."

Hank still wasn't saying anything; he just sat there on the edge of the couch, puffing on his cigar and hanging on Graham's every word.

She put the cap back on her pen and pushed her chair away from the desk. "Well, Mr. Graham," she said, rising to her feet, "I'm afraid that without references, we simply couldn't consider you for the job."

He got to his feet and stared at her across the desk. "I never said I didn't have references." How he managed to remain so technically polite yet so threatening at the same time baffled her.

"When you said your work was top secret, I assumed—"

That dazzling smile was back. "Never assume, Ms. Wiley. Assumptions can get you in all kinds of trouble."

She didn't return the smile. The man was altogether too sure of himself.

She decided to try another approach, one that, at the very least, would knock him back on his self-confident heels.

"I'm afraid we were looking for someone with a music background, Mr. Graham." She found it difficult to hold back her smile. "Nothing in your—" she paused "—verbal résumé indicates the proper requirements." The fact that it didn't matter if the driver knew a G clef from a G-string was incidental. Now, if Hank just kept his mouth shut, they could knock off the rest of the interviews and be at dinner, tucked away in Hank's private suite at the Golden Nugget, within the hour.

"I know a little about music," Tony Graham said.

The man really had no shame. Couldn't he recognize an impolite brush-off when he heard it? "So you know a little about music, do you?" *Listen, pal, playing "Chopsticks" with help doesn't count.*

Graham leaned across the desk. "Try me."

She sat back down and leaned back in her chair, adopting her best executive demeanor. "Liszt," she said. *Make my day: say grocery.*

"Who composed the *Hungarian Rhapsodies*?"

Okay, so he listened to *Readers Digest* record albums. "Sonata."

"What is a musical composition in three or four movements?"

Lucky guess.

She dug way back into her storehouse of music trivia. "Georges Sand."

"Who was Chopin's mistr—"

"Good God!" Hank exploded from the sofa. "What in hell are we doin', playin' *Jeopardy*? This is a job interview, girl, not some game show."

Jill, who had been having a terrific time, glared at her grandfather. "Mind your own business, old man. This is my part of the deal, not yours."

"Don't call him 'old man,'" Tony said. "Show some respect."

Jill glared at him this time. "Maybe you're the one who should mind his own business."

"Is this going to be my business?" He still seemed as comfortable as if he were lounging on a beach somewhere. "Do I get the job?"

"No," said Jill.

"Yes," said her grandfather.

"It's up to me," she said. "I'm the one who'll have to spend twenty-four hours a day with him."

Graham perked up. "Twenty-four?"

"Figuratively speaking." She didn't know exactly why it had happened, but it was obvious she'd never regained control of the interview. From the second she saw Tony Graham standing in the doorway she'd been far too aware of him as a man to deal with him as a prospective employee. No matter how liberated she liked to think of herself, she was still a sucker for a gorgeous face.

The thing to do now was regroup her forces and beat a valiant retreat.

"This has been a fascinating interview, Mr. Graham, but I think it's time to say good-night."

"Better have him fill out a withholdin' form first," Hank said, shaking Graham's extended hand. "With these damn new tax laws, we want to be walkin' on the straight and narrow."

Graham, that louse, beamed. "I couldn't agree with you more, sir."

Oh, no, you don't, she thought. *Not even a show of male solidarity is going to force me into anything.*

She extended her hand toward Tony Graham. "Thank you and goodbye."

He stared at her blankly, that infernal air of self-confidence finally cracking. "Should I come back tomorrow and fill out the paperwork?"

"What paperwork?"

He glanced at Hank then back at her. "Tax statements, references, the usual."

"If you get the job, you can come back." She managed to ignore her grandfather's scowl.

"You mean I haven't been given the job yet?"

"I mean, you haven't been given the job at all."

She watched, fascinated, as the first flicker of vulnerability sputtered then died. So he was human after all.

The balance of power shifted back to her.

He was, however, still one hell of a tough customer. "I'm staying at Caesar's," he said. "You can reach me there until Thursday morning."

And with a nod in Hank's direction, he turned and left.

She and her grandfather were silent until they heard the creak of the elevator doors sliding shut after the world's most independent job applicant.

"Forget it," Jill said before Hank could utter a word. "He's all wrong for the job." If Graham handled work the way he handled interviews, she'd be the one hauling the baby grand from town to town.

Hank whipped out a silver penknife and flicked a pebble from the sole of his left boot. "Don't think you're gonna find none better."

"There are still three more applicants," she said, sifting through the remaining forms. "One of them has to fill the bill."

"One already has."

"If you like him so damn much, Pa, why don't you hire him?"

"If I needed a truck driver I would, girl. You wouldn't stand a chance."

She had to hand it to her grandfather; he could take it with the best of them—which was fortunate since she intended to dish it out.

"Did you see the way he was dressed?" she muttered. "Deck shoes in Nevada. Who was he trying to kid?"

"You sound like an Eastern snob," Hank shot back. "You never heard of Lake Mead? Besides, the man's not even from these parts." He plucked Graham's improvised application from the rejected pile. "Says here he's from New York."

"That proves my point. If he's from New York, what's he doing out here looking for a job?"

"Times are tough all over, girl. A man sometimes has to travel to find work."

"Well, he's going to have to keep on trucking," she said as she buzzed Emily to bring in the next applicant, "because I have a feeling this next guy is going to be Mr. Right."

WRONG AGAIN.

The next guy wasn't Mr. Right, or Mr. Nearly-Right, or Mr. Close-But-No-Cigar.

And neither were the two bozos who came after him, one of whom had better taste in earrings and eye make-up than she did.

By the time she and Hank got to the Golden Nugget and were seated in front of two gorgeous sirloin steaks, she was exhausted, confused and ready to call the whole thing off.

"I can't believe it," she said, making quick work of a stack of onion rings. "A huge, macho state like Nevada and I can't find one normal human male to drive a truck."

Hank said nothing, just cut into his steak.

"There has to be someone out there who can do it," she said, fiddling with her glass of beer.

Hank still said nothing.

"I still have two more days to look around for a good driver."

Hank didn't even remind her that her help-wanted ad had been canceled and she had no more applicants to see.

She popped a French fry into her mouth and sighed. "It's Graham, isn't it? He's won by default."

"Well, girl," said her grandfather, reaching for the Heinz ketchup. "I think you've finally come to your senses."

And finally met her match.

Chapter Two

Antony Graham Wellington IV was hard put to pin-point exactly when it happened, but by the time he got back to his penthouse suite at Caesar's Palace, getting that job with Jill Wiley had become a matter of honor.

And, for a change, it wasn't Wellington family honor that worried him: It was his own.

He thought he'd breeze into that office and walk off with the job in ten seconds flat. It had never occurred to him that there would be any other outcome.

It hadn't occurred to him that she wouldn't want to hire him.

And it sure as hell hadn't occurred to him that she wouldn't even like him.

Unbelievable.

He entered the living room of the four-bedroom suite, stripped off his polo shirt and tossed it over the back of a gilt-and-rococo side chair.

Strange, he thought as he poured Scotch into a chunky Baccarat tumbler and stretched out on the *faux* Louis XIV sofa that was the height of Vegas chic. More than strange.

By the time Jill Wiley said "Don't call me, I'll call you," getting that job had become more than a matter of winning a Silver Shadow.

It was a matter of pride.

Doubt had been etched all over that beautiful porcelain face of hers. Distrust had colored every question she threw his way.

Jill Wiley didn't think he could cut it.

He took a long slug of Scotch and grimaced.

She might have a point there.

Walking into that office as just plain Tony Graham, without the shield of money and position that had been his birthright for twenty-eight years, had been harder than he ever could have guessed.

The people he dealt with in his daily life knew everything there was to know about him, from his family's pedigree to the growth in his stock options, to the status of his current romance. He was accustomed to speaking in a verbal shorthand understood only by those who had grown up as "old money."

Doors always opened wide for him. So when he found himself knocking for the first time, he wasn't altogether sure he liked the feeling.

What the hell difference did it make anyway, he thought as he polished off the Scotch. It didn't matter how odd he felt—he wasn't about to get the job.

In fact, if he didn't think the notion was paranoid and bordering on psychic nonsense, he would have believed Jill Wiley saw right through him.

Now *that* was ridiculous.

He got up to get another Scotch.

There was no way a woman who earned her living playing piano in backwater towns for culture-starved ranchers could see through him. Sure, he'd hit a few wrong notes during their interview but nothing that would give him away. Maybe if he had only—

Fortunately the telephone cut his pathetic conjectures short.

Unfortunately it was his father on the other end.

"Did you get the job?"

Tony poured an extra finger of Scotch into the tumbler.

"Antony, stop drinking and answer me. I've been thinking a great deal about that new Rolls you're going to give me."

"A 1932 Silver Shadow," Tony said, dodging the bullet. "Who'd want a new one?"

"I do," Mr. Wellington said. "And when I win, I fully expect you to comply with my wishes. Now, answer me: Did you or did you not get the job?"

"They're still interviewing."

"Interesting." His father's laugh was altogether too hearty. "So they weren't bowled over by your Wellington charm?"

"Did you forget the ground rules?" Tony countered, feeling both annoyed and defensive. "I'm doing this without benefit of the illustrious Wellington name. You should try it sometime."

"I'm not the one railing against reality, Antony. I have no problem with who and what I am. If only you—"

"This is old territory, Dad."

"Perhaps, but we seem to find ourselves here often enough, don't we?"

Not tonight.

Tony's relationship with his father was more complex than either one was comfortable acknowledging, a fact that had made things rocky from time to time over the years.

He had grown up with a well-developed sense of lineage but no feeling for what it meant to be part of a family. His mother had died before his first birthday, and the elder Wellington had turned his life over to the continuation of the Wellington family fortune. The continuation of the family—namely, Antony IV—had been assigned to a series of nannies, prep schools and Yale professors.

Once he was old enough, Antony IV had turned his life over to the pursuit of pleasure. Happiness was something neither man gave much thought to; neither one really believed it possible.

In his father, Tony saw ambition and determination—all the wonderful Wellington character traits that had mysteriously skipped his generation.

In Tony, his father saw every mistake he'd ever made.

The last thing Tony needed was a lecture on noblesse oblige and the rightful place of the wealthy in American society—not to mention what color interior his father wanted in his new Rolls Royce.

Going home a loser would be tough enough. The least his father could do was wait until he got there before he started rubbing it in.

Tony ended the conversation before an argument did and was reaching for the room service menu when the phone rang again.

"Give it a rest, Dad," he said in lieu of greeting. "At least wait until I land at JFK before you start in on me again."

Silence. Then: "Mr. Graham?"

His stomach knotted. He'd have to start watching the Scotch; it was beginning to get to him.

"Mr. Graham?" He knew it before she said it: "This is Jill Wiley."

"I thought you were my father."

"So I gathered."

"Is there something I can do for you?" *Better watch that.* He was sounding like a Wellington again. "You want something?"

"Upon careful consideration I've decided we need to hold a more extensive interview."

"I'm free tomorrow morning." And every morning, not that it was any of her business.

"I was thinking more in terms of tonight."

"Tonight?"

"Yes. That is, if you can make it."

He glanced at his watch. It was a little after seven. The night lay before him like a barren stretch of desert highway. "I still have to eat dinner," he said, stalling. "I don't know how long it'll take me to get back to your office."

"You won't have to come back to the office, Mr. Graham. I'd be glad to meet you at your hotel."

"I don't mind coming back to the office, Ms. Wiley." What dialogue, he thought. They sounded like rejects from *Masterpiece Theatre Goes to Las Vegas*.

"That won't be necessary, Mr. Graham." A pause, followed by an uncertain—but very appealing—laugh. "I'm calling from the lobby."

The Silver Shadow was in the bag.

WHERE WAS HE?

Jill had been toying with a piña colada the size of a punch bowl for fifteen minutes, while she waited for the enigmatic Tony Graham to show up.

When he'd suggested they meet at Cleopatra's Barge, one of the hotel's snazzier bars, she hadn't thought anything of it. He was staying in the hotel, after all. How long could it take for him to get down to the lobby to meet her?

Certainly she was sophisticated enough to fend off the attentions of a few amorous toothpaste salesmen while she waited.

Well, guess again.

Jill had badly underestimated the toothpaste salesmen of this country. From the second she made her way via gangplank over the mini-Nile encircling the barge, she'd been fair game. Men lurked behind ostrich-feather fans and statues of the ancient pharaohs, waiting to strike like Cleopatra's asp. In fact, if Uncle Sam had been able to harness their single-mindedness to a higher purpose, World War II would have been over a week after Pearl Harbor.

She'd tried being polite. She'd tried being blunt. She'd even followed Nancy Reagan's advice and just said no. Nothing, it seemed, could sway these goal-oriented entrepreneurs from success.

She took a seat in a plush royal-purple booth with a clear view of the entrance—and the exit—and found herself suddenly more popular than chocolate-chip cookies on a fat farm.

So this was what being single in the eighties was all about? No wonder computer dating and personal ads were so popular.

Hank had been right. Her life in Palm Beach was insular, a tightly woven network of family and old friends who tried to shield her from the normal vicissitudes of existence. No one, of course, had been able to shield her from her travesty of a marriage or the tragedy of losing her baby—and her ability to bear another one.

She probably would have one day stumbled into a marriage with Tyler Austin simply as a hedge against the loneliness that built within her with each month that passed.

Of course, this idea of her grandfather's was insane. The logistics of being a one-woman traveling philharmonic was enough to boggle the mind, but damned if the temptation to hit the road didn't grow more enticing with every moment.

Music had been the one constant in her life, the one thing that made her feel special. Neither of her parents understood music as anything but a backdrop for dinner conversation, but they did take pride in her accomplishments—however minor they may have been—and, God, how hard she had tried to please.

Her ex-husband had dismissed her talent; Tyler Austin ignored it.

Hank was the only one who truly understood.

"Why, Pa?" she had asked him the night he challenged her with his idea. "Why are you doing this?"

"Because you're slidin' headfirst toward another disaster, girl, and I'll be damned if I sit back and watch you disappear into respectability. I kept my mouth shut once but never again."

"We're not all outlaws like you. Some of us were born to play by the rules." Her very existence in the Von Eron family was predicated on rules and regulations and legal documents all neatly signed and dated and tucked away in some dank and musty safety deposit vault.

"Not you," he had said. "You been special since the day you were born, girl, and I'll see hellfire before I let you waste yourself on a slug like Tyler Austin."

"This can all backfire, you realize?" She hadn't been able to disguise the enthusiasm building inside her. "I might end up playing for a herd of longhorns."

"Can't be no worse than playin' for your ma's garden club."

"I must be crazy. It sounds wonderful."

"Wildness runs in the family, girl. You can't escape it."

"I'm adopted, Pa."

"Don't matter. You're more like me than my own flesh and blood."

She thought of the child she'd lost and of all the dreams she'd lost along with it.

"You'd make a wonderful great-grandfather," she said softly. "I wish I'd been able to carry that child." That tiny life would have been her connection with the future, her gift to Agneta and Bill Von Eron who had taken her in and created a place for her in their lives where none had existed before. That baby would have been Hank's lifeline into the future for, while Wiley blood wouldn't flow in the child's veins, Jill would have made certain the Wiley spirit did.

"Don't waste time wishin' for things that can't be," he said, his voice gruff but not unkind. "Go out and take what you can."

And so there she was a few weeks later, sipping her second piña colada, ready to call an end to the whole thing and catch a cab back to her grandfather's hotel suite in abject defeat because she'd been stood up by the only man in Nevada who didn't wear a pound of gold around his neck.

Through her peripheral vision she saw a man approaching her. He stopped in front of her booth but she refused to look up and make eye contact. If she saw one more man wearing a gold rope flea collar, she wouldn't be held responsible for her actions.

"Don't say anything," she hissed. "Just keep your suggestions to yourself and find someone else."

She stared intently at the tiny orange-and-pink parasol suspended in her piña colada.

The man didn't move.

"I mean business," she said. "Go away." Thank God for the time she'd spent studying music in New York. Palm Beach certainly didn't prepare a woman for situations like this.

"You're a lot tougher than you look, Ms. Wiley."

She groaned into a pineapple spear. "Don't tell me," she said, covering her eyes. "Tony Graham, isn't it?"

He slid into the booth across from her, smelling of soap and a trace of Scotch. He gestured toward the horde of men lining the bar. "The lions giving you a tough time?"

Oh, no, you don't, she thought. *You're not going to turn things around on me again.* "Nothing I can't handle," she said as a toga-clad waitress sidled up to him and batted her impossibly long, obviously fake eyelashes in his direction.

He ordered a Perrier with a twist and somehow managed to keep his Roman nose out of the waitress's cleavage—which was no small accomplishment.

"I'm not offended by hard liquor, Mr. Graham," she said, "just as long as it's not behind the wheel of my truck. Besides, I've already smelled the Scotch on your breath, so there's no point pretending to be a teetotaler."

"I'm not pretending to be anything." He popped a cashew in his mouth. "I've already had a couple of drinks, and now it's time for Perrier." He nodded as the waitress deposited his mineral water in front of him. "It's also none of your business."

"If I hire you to be my driver, it's my business."

He leaned back in his seat, all male arrogance and splendor. A dangerous combination, the same combination that had attracted her to her ex-husband a thousand lifetimes ago.

"You haven't hired me yet," he pointed out. "But I'm assuming that's what this meeting is leading up to."

"Don't make assumptions, Mr. Graham," she said, tipping the power balance back toward her side. "They can have a way of tripping you up."

His confident smile faded, and he put his hands palm up on the table. "Look, Ms. Wiley, it's been a long day, and I still haven't had dinner. If you feel like playing psychological power games, that's your business, but you're going to have to find someone else to be your opponent." He slid out of the booth and stood up. "It's been nice," he said, "but I'm out of here."

Before she could think of a retort—witty or otherwise—he crossed the gangplank and disappeared.

Face flaming, Jill yanked a twenty-dollar bill out of her purse, tossed it on the tabletop and dashed off after him. He was checking the menu on the window of The Bacchanal when she caught up with him.

"We haven't finished our discussion," she said, following him past two imposing golden lions who guarded the entrance and the lighted pool.

The maitre d' approached them. "How many, sir?"

"One," said Tony Graham.

"Two," said Jill.

The maitre d' admirably managed to keep a straight face as he led the way to a corner table near an elaborate marble fountain complete with wood nymphs, satyrs and one very voluptuous Venus.

Tony Graham waited until the man was out of earshot before he spoke. "Join me for dinner, why don't you?"

"There's no need for sarcasm. You're the one who walked out, not me."

"It was walk out or knock you flat. You want me to reconsider?"

"You have a quick temper."

He met her eyes. "Not usually. You seem to bring out the best in me."

She sighed and sank into the banquette. "Do you think we could erase the last half hour and try again? This isn't exactly the way I had things planned."

He waved away the wine steward and flipped open his menu. "I'm game if you are."

"Listen." She leaned forward. "I'm in a bind. My tour starts in four days, and I still don't have a driver." She waited for him to say something. It was perfectly obvious she was going to offer him the job; the least he could do was make it easy for her.

He didn't.

"Damn it," she said. "You've got the job.'

"Thanks." He motioned the waiter over to take his order. "I don't want it."

"Okay. I guess I deserved that. Let me rephrase it: I'm offering you the job, Mr. Graham."

"And I'm refusing it."

She forced a smile. "Very funny, but the joke's over."

"I'm not joking, Ms. Wiley. In case you haven't noticed, we don't seem to be getting along. What in hell do you think would happen if we had to spend twenty-four hours a day together? We haven't even been able to get through a job interview. Thanks, but no thanks."

"If I had the energy, I'd try to change your mind, but I'm too exhausted." She opened her menu then peered at him over the top. "Do you mind if I grab something to eat?"

"Be my guest." That smile of his reappeared. "I mean that figuratively, of course."

"Of course." Her own smile surprised them both.

The waiter materialized next to their table. Tony ordered goose liver Strasbourg and salmon braised in champagne, and Jill whistled softly in admiration. Her own tastes ran toward chicken, which was exactly what she ordered.

"I must be crazy," she said, sipping a glass of rosé wine served by a slave girl in an abbreviated harem outfit. "This is my second dinner tonight. Stress does terrible things to my appetite."

"You don't look any the worse for the wear."

"A compliment, Mr. Graham? How far we've come."

"What the hell," he said, refilling her glass. "Now that we both know we'll never see each other again, we can let it all hang out."

"I haven't heard anyone say 'let it all hang out' since I graduated high school."

"Too bad we won't be working together, then. Think of all the vocabulary lessons you could have."

"Listen," she said, taking another sip of rosé, "right now that seems a small price to pay to have a driver. I'm getting desperate."

"I'll let that insult pass."

She groaned. "I didn't mean that the way it sounded. I'm just too tired to be articulate."

"You had a pretty good crowd waiting when I left," he said as the waiter brought their salads. "No luck?"

"Not a bit. Would you believe the last one dyed his eyebrows to match his nail polish?"

That knockout smile of his widened. "I haven't heard anyone say 'Would you believe' since the last *Get Smart* festival was on TV."

Jill winced and picked up her fork. "I had that coming, didn't I?"

"You did. That was too good an opening."

She speared a tomato with her fork. "If you'd seen Clarence O'Day, you wouldn't be so hard on me."

"What was wrong with Clarence O'Day?"

"Hair," she said, popping the tomato into her mouth.

"Hair's a criminal offense these days?"

She shivered. "In your ears, it is."

Tony Graham stared at her. "He didn't get the job because of that?"

"There has to be some criteria for making a decision. I couldn't imagine riding mile after mile across the Nevada desert with a man who looks like Cheetah."

"I see your point. What was wrong with the others?"

She fished out an anchovy and put it on the side of her bread plate. "You name it—everything from bad breath to a prison record to terminal stupidity. I'm beginning to think I'll have to do the driving myself."

He grinned and swiped her anchovy. "You'll find somebody. There's bound to be a few decent males left in Vegas."

She shot him a look. "I *did* find somebody, Mr. Graham. You turned me down."

"Dangerous territory," he said, laughing. "Why don't we declare a moratorium on the subject during dinner?"

They shook hands on it, and Jill was surprised to find Tony Graham to be great company when she wasn't trying to convince him to come to work for her and he wasn't telling her, in more polite terms, to go to hell.

They compared notes on Woody Allen and Evelyn Waugh, on Beethoven and Brahms and Billy Idol. He was opinionated, witty, and each time he opened his mouth, he shattered another of her misconceptions.

Their waiter poured them each a cup of espresso then moved discreetly away.

"You realize you're not at all the way I expected a truck driver to be."

He looked up from the amaretto cheesecake he was attacking. "What were you expecting?"

"I told you about the other applicants."

"And that's what you figured I'd be like?"

"There was no reason to think you'd be any different."

"I hope I've changed your mind about truck drivers."

"You have." She took a long sip of the coffee. "I only wish I could change your mind about taking the job."

Another huge forkful of cheesecake disappeared into his mouth. "Question," he said. "What makes you think ranchers and farmers and small-town types want to hear you and your Steinway?"

"Bornsdorfer," she corrected, "and I know for a fact there's an audience out there." She rummaged in her briefcase and plucked out the itinerary Hank had put together. "See?" She handed it to him. "Two weeks of engagements and that's just a start."

He flipped through it then handed it back to her. "Do you think you'll end up working at least a month?"

She shrugged. "No reason to think otherwise. This is a huge country, Tony, and there are a lot of people who've never once heard live music."

"You're not going to make much money playing in high school gymnasiums and town halls."

"I know that."

"With the salary you're offering me, I'd be surprised if you broke even."

"That's *my* problem."

"I don't get it, Jill. If it's not the money, what is it?"

She thought about the sharply sensual pleasure of filling a room with music and the years of love and training that had, so far, amounted to nothing—intensely personal reasons that she had barely even touched on with Hank, much less with a total stranger.

"I don't think I could explain it to you." She looked down. She wasn't sure she could explain it to herself.

"I'm interested," he said, tilting her chin up so she was forced to meet his eyes. "I'd like to understand."

What could it hurt? They'd never see each other again; talking to Tony Graham, a perfect stranger, was as safe as the confessional. What the hell. Maybe it was the combination of the two piña coladas and some rosé, but this time tomorrow she'd be back in Palm Beach at the Lake Worth Cultural Museum Charity Ball and Tony Graham would be who-knew-where and she really wanted to talk to someone who didn't make judgments based on love.

"It's really pretty simple," she said. "I attended Juilliard, won a scholarship to the Mozarteum in Austria, was named Most Promising Young Pianist of 1981 and I married a man who thought a woman's place was in the home.'' Preferably the nursery, but that was another story.

"And you finally had enough?''

"No.'' This was the hard part. "He finally had enough. He married a woman twice as rich, three years older and four months pregnant. Craig actually did quite well for himself.''

"And you?''

"It took a while, but I'm fine. I never thought I'd say this, but I may even give marriage another go someday.'' She saw his glance shift to her left ring finger. "Not yet. I said someday.''

"Anyone particular in mind?''

Tyler Austin popped into her brain for the first time that day. "Let's say someone has me in mind. Right now all I can think of is finding a driver and hitting the road. Speaking of which—'' she leaned across the table and looked at his watch ''—my car should be outside.''

"Your car?''

Damn. She really was feeling indiscreet tonight. "My grandfather said he'd send his car over at eleven. I really have to get going.''

She pulled out her American Express card to pay the bill at the same moment Tony Graham whipped out his wallet.

"It's on me,'' she said. "I'm the one who dragged you out for this meeting.''

"No. I had to eat anyway.''

They split the cost; Jill paid with plastic and Tony reimbursed her in cash. He walked her out to the lobby.

"That's a great Rolex knockoff you're wearing," she said as they passed three women in spangled spandex who obviously worked evenings. "It fooled me there for a second."

He looked down at his watch as if he'd never really seen it before. "Yeah," he said. "It is a good one, isn't it?"

She glanced out the front door and saw Hank's vintage Caddy limo waiting near the curb.

"Well, Tony Graham," she said, extending her right hand. "I hope you find the job you're looking for."

"Well, Jill Wiley," he said as her hand disappeared in his, "I think I already have."

Chapter Three

Jill stared at him, her mind an absolute blank. "What?"

He smiled. "When do I start, boss?"

"You're kidding, aren't you?"

"The job is still open, isn't it?"

"Well, yes, but I thought we already decided that—"

"You did offer it to me less than an hour ago, didn't you?"

"You know I did, but—"

"I'll take it."

"But you said you didn't want it."

"I've changed my mind."

"I thought that was a woman's prerogative."

"A sexist statement from an independent woman?"

"You're dead serious, aren't you?" Despite the twinkle in his eyes, she knew he meant business.

"Never more serious."

"What changed your mind?"

An indefinable expression passed across his face and was gone before she could analyze it. How had she forgotten how handsome he was?

"You did."

Quickly she reviewed all of the enticements that were part of the package. "The health insurance? The travel? What?"

"The itinerary. Any Juilliard grad who's willing to play Paiute Hollow deserves a truck driver who knows Liszt from Tchaikovsky."

"The work might be boring for you," she said, suddenly frightened now that it looked as if it were really going to happen after all. "Are you sure?"

"Last chance, lady. Am I hired or not?"

He was a far cry from the hirsute Clarence O'Day, she'd grant him that. And a truck driver didn't have to be sixty years old and out of shape, did he?

"Why not?" she said. "You're hired."

A huge smile broke across his face. "So when do we start? We have to outfit the truck, plot our route, book hotel space—"

Fred, her grandfather's driver, got out and leaned against the hood of the ancient Caddy. "Gotta get back, Jilly," he yelled. "The old man wants the car tonight."

Tony looked at his watch. "It's almost midnight. Your grandfather is going out?"

"Don't ask. He didn't find five wives by staying home next to the fireplace."

Graham laughed. "I'd like to get to know him better."

"You will." She adjusted the collar of her jacket and grinned up at him. "Starting tomorrow."

"He'll be helping us get ready?"

"Not us, Tony. You."

"Me?"

She handed him a slip of paper with a hangar number at nearby McCarran Airport scribbled on it. "Tomorrow morning, nine sharp. Pa hates lateness so be on time."

"You'll be there, too?"

"Afraid not."

"Just me and your grandfather?"

"Until Sunday."

"That's a hell of a thing to do to me."

"Better get used to it," she said, laughing, "because I'm even tougher than he is." A lie, but better to establish who was boss right up front. "Having second thoughts?" The look on his face was priceless.

"Hell, no. Tomorrow morning at nine. I'll be there."

She was still smiling as the Caddy pulled away and headed back downtown.

TONY STOOD IN THE DOORWAY and watched as the huge-finned Caddy whisked Jill Wiley away.

A swarm of tourists, bound for Cosby's second show, whizzed past him in a cloud of Old Spice and Arpège and Pepto Bismol. He barely noticed them. He was still trying to take in what had just happened.

He had a job.

A real job. A job with a boss he wasn't related to and W-2 forms and insurance plans and every other thing that he had not one damned bit of experience dealing with.

Incredible.

That tiny woman with the full head of pale blond curls and the big gray eyes that shimmered like polished pewter was his boss.

Unbelievable.

What was really unbelievable was the fact that he *had* a boss. The whole thing had started out as a kind of rich man's lark, a pointed joke between his father and him that had as much to do with punching a time clock as it did with the Rolls Royce.

Two years ago, in an attempt to stave off an attack of terminal boredom, he'd taken over control of the trucking firm his mother had left in trust for him when she died.

He'd quickly discovered that Yale hadn't done as good a job of preparing him for reality as Ivy Leaguers liked to believe. Totally at a loss for dealing equably with both unions and upper-level management, he'd tried to juggle his social life with his business responsibilities, and AGW Trucking quickly sank into financial oblivion, disappearing beneath a flood of tax write-offs. Not once had he thought of the hundreds of people thrown out of work by his laissez-faire attitude toward the company.

He'd gone west to make a statement about the lifestyle of the very rich, but he'd never stopped long enough to think about the other people who would become involved along the way.

Jill Wiley, for instance.

This whole thing meant something to her. Only a total fool would have missed that look in her eyes as she talked about her music.

About her marriage.

The straightforward, no-nonsense way she approached the undertaking was radically different from the way he usually did things, and he found himself seeing past her beauty in a way that shocked the hell out of him.

It wasn't as if he'd lied to her, exactly. He had owned a company. It had been involved in some government work, and he did own some rental property in Cold Spring Harbor, even though he'd never once lived in it.

Why then did that grave look in her beautiful eyes unnerve him so? Why did the Rolls Royce suddenly seem so unimportant?

He leaned against the people mover that carried an endless stream of tourists to and from Caesar's and looked at his watch. Eight hours until he reported for duty. Still time to catch a late show or spend a few bucks at the blackjack table.

"Pa hates lateness," Jill had said, "so be on time."

He thought of the old man's bone-crushing grip and Jill's disarming bluntness and shrugged.

"What the hell," he said out loud, wheeling back toward the hotel. If he was going to play the working man, there was no time like the present to start. Get a good night's sleep, report to the old man on the stroke of nine, and work his butt off for the next thirty days.

An easy way to earn a Silver Shadow—and show his father and the other Emory Club denizens that there was more to life than cheating at poker.

A month?

Piece of cake.

Maybe he'd even learn what made Jill Wiley tick.

"YOU'RE LATE."

Tony squinted into the sun in the general direction of the man's voice. "Mr. Wiley?"

"Who the hell else you expectin', Graham? Ronald Reagan?" The old man came out of the hangar, planted himself directly in front of Tony. "Why are you late?"

Tony looked at the Bulova he'd bought to replace the pricey Rolex that had nearly blown his cover. Nine on the nose. "You sure your watch isn't fast?"

Wiley took a long drag on a cigar and eyed Tony. "Pretty sure of yourself, ain't you, Graham?"

Testing him, was he? "Yeah," Tony said, taking a step to the right so Wiley was the one now facing into the sunshine. "Is that a problem?" Wellingtons hadn't amassed millions by not knowing how to take advantage of most situations.

Wiley looked at him long and hard through a cloud of acrid cigar smoke. "I don't rightly know. Depends on how you feel about hard work."

Now this was going to be a tough one. "Hard work doesn't bother me." He would have figured on at least one bolt of lightning after a statement like that. Hell, he might as well go all the way. "That cigar of yours is another story." He waved his hand in front of his nose. "Frankly, Wiley, it stinks."

The old man's jaw dropped open, and the cigar teetered precariously on his upper lip. "You always shoot your mouth off like that?"

"Afraid so." No sense lying about that. He'd already done the damage. Besides, some things you just couldn't hide. "Is *that* going to be a problem?"

"Let me tell you something, Graham." Hank Wiley draped an arm across Tony's shoulders, and Tony could feel the power in those gnarled fingers. "I got no problem with a man speakin' his mind. I been known to sound off a time or two myself." He paused for the answering chuckle that Tony had no trouble supplying. "What I got a problem with is my granddaughter." The iron grip tightened. "You do anything to hurt that gal and you're gonna have me to answer to." The old man's voice was fierce as the desert sun. "You understand what I'm sayin' to you, Graham?"

In an unmistakable show of strength, Tony politely pulled away from the man's grasp and looked him straight in the eye. "I understand what you're saying,

Wiley." A vision of Jill, blond and small and lovely, swirled past his eyes. A damn shame but unavoidable. "You don't have to worry. All I'm looking for is a job."

The old man started to draw in on his cigar once more then suddenly stubbed it out.

Tony grinned.

Hank's eyes twinkled but he didn't crack a smile.

"What're you lookin' at, Graham?" he bellowed. "You been standin' there wastin' my time and money for fifteen minutes now. Let's get it in gear."

"I'm waiting on you, Wiley. Lead the way."

The old man was halfway around the side of the hangar before Tony had gone six feet.

It was going to be one hell of a day.

"DAMN!" Jill leaned forward toward the mirror above her dressing table. Two nails broken and she still hadn't managed to unclasp her necklace.

"Need some help, darling?" Her mother's voice wafted across the room.

"Desperately!" Jill made a face at her own reflection. "Aunt Edith's pearls are about to become a permanent fixture."

Agneta Von Eron, formerly Agnes Wiley of Silver Spur, rustled into her daughter's bedroom, all taffeta skirts and Chanel No 5. "The clasp on Edie's pearls has always been a bother." She rested a hand on Jill's shoulder. "Let me."

Jill lifted her hair off her neck and dipped her head forward as her mother deftly undid the troublesome clasp.

"There," said Agneta, catching the string of perfectly matched pearls between her long fingers. "Nothing to it."

"I can handle an étude with the best of them," Jill said, shaking her head. "Why should a simple clasp be such a problem?"

Agneta settled herself on the chaise longue by the French doors and gracefully arranged her voluminous skirts around her. "One of the many mysteries of life, darling. I am good with jewelry. You, however, were given other gifts."

"Ah, yes." Jill picked up her hairbrush and drew it slowly through her hair. "Is this the prelude to 'The Lecture'?"

"You're rushing things, Jillian." An amused smile played at the corners of Agneta's perfectly lipsticked mouth. "I was going to lead ever-so-stylishly into it."

Everything Agneta Von Eron did, she did with style. Jill's earliest memories were of her beautiful mother dispatching the servants with a smile and a wave of her hand, of charming William with just one look from those huge, deep blue eyes. It was a testament to her strong will—and her desire to be accepted by Bill's family—that no signs of Agnes Wiley peeked through her impeccable exterior. Not even when Hank blew into town with his Cuban cigars and endless cussing and his infernal habit of calling her "Aggie-girl," did her origins show. Hank had made his fortune in the forties, but Agneta was determined to behave as if Wiley money had preceded the Pilgrims by a century or two.

Jill had always loved it when her grandfather called her mother Aggie because that old down-home name was drastically at odds with the Agneta Von Eron who understood all that was inherently mysterious: Agneta knew why pearl necklaces should be comprised of odd-numbered strands. She had mastered the mystery of eighteen-button gloves and the ritual surrounding the proper consumption of asparagus hollandaise at a formal dinner.

From the very beginning Agneta had made it her business to understand the ins and outs of high-society pomp and circumstance and she had used that knowledge to smooth her daughter's entrance into that world. Agneta was very aware of the difference between old money and painfully new and she was determined her only child would fit in with the old.

As a child, Jill had been dressed in the de rigeur gingham dresses with the ubiquitous smocking; she had a closet floor filled with black patent Mary Janes and a drawerful of perfect, white anklets. When the family traveled north to see Aunt Edith or Grandmere Juliana, she was dressed in her pale blue wool coat with the black velvet collar.

Agneta made certain her only child went to Miss Porter's School. She arranged for ballet lessons and ballroom dancing lessons and endless hours perfecting social graces no normal woman would ever need.

And Jillian Von Eron, heiress to the Von Eron millions, had turned everything upside down the first day she walked into Madame Teruschenkov's studio and touched the smooth, ivory keys of her teacher's ancient Steinway.

Now, a certain level of music mastery was considered necessary to the proper upbringing of a fine Palm Beach daughter, and, at first, Agneta and William had been pleased with their daughter's precocious abilities.

Quickly, however, their pride turned to bemusement, then shock as their beautiful girl began to talk about a career as a concert pianist.

Careers simply weren't necessary among their class. Wasn't there enough to do with debutante parties and charity work and the all-encompassing task of finding the proper husband? A good marriage was really the first and foremost occupation of every girl over sixteen—or it certainly should be.

And that was where Agneta Von Eron revealed her true self: both Agneta Von Eron and Agnes Wiley believed in love.

Romantic love.

The kind that came with hearts and flowers and violins and big fat cupids with love-tipped arrows.

Agneta subscribed to the notions of love at first sight, love across a crowded room and a love for all time. The very first moment she saw William Von Eron striding across the campus at Princeton University, she forgot all about her father's grandiose plans for her future and her studies and even how to put one foot in front of the other.

She fell in love.

Fortunately, William Von Eron felt the same, and their union had survived three decades, seven presidents and more formal dinners than any couple should be required to sit through.

And Jill was the perfect product of her environment.

Not even her time in Juilliard and the Mozarteum in Vienna was enough to make her break with romantic tradition. The moment she fell in love with Craig Wyatt of the Delaware Wyatts, music slid to second place. She had a wedding to plan and a household to set up and a whole wonderful future as a wife and mother ahead of her. How could she go from city to city as a concert pianist with so many responsibilities?

No matter how much she loved music, she still had loved Craig more. Giving up her own dreams seemed a small enough sacrifice in order to create a family with someone as wonderful as he.

Fate—and her beloved husband—unfortunately had other ideas.

Ideas that had spelled an end to their marriage before their third anniversary and an end to romantic dreaming.

"You're being as rude to me as you were to Tyler, Jillian." Her mother's voice lasered in on her. "Am I boring you so?"

Jill snapped back to attention. "No, Mother, of course not. I was just wondering why I never managed to pick up some of the social graces that come so easily to you."

Agneta took off her diamond-and-ruby earring and massaged her left earlobe. "You never cared to."

"Mother!"

Agneta laughed at Jill's mock outrage. "I speak the truth, Jillian. You had no interest in any of it. Your talent is the piano; mine is arranging place settings."

Jill put her brush down on the dressing table and faced her mother. Might as well get it all out in the open. "You want to lecture me about Tyler, don't you?"

Her mother sighed and replaced her earring. "Always rushing things, aren't you, darling? I wish you'd allow me to lead into delicate topics with at least a small degree of finesse."

"Sometimes it's difficult for me to believe you're Hank's daughter."

"Sometimes it's difficult for me, as well, but you're avoiding the issue, daughter mine."

"I'd hoped you hadn't noticed."

"As you said, details are my forte." She reached over and took Jill's hand. "Why are you doing this crazy thing, Jillian? Tyler won't wait forever for you."

Her mother's fingers were long and beautifully shaped, much like Jill's own, but the similarity was an accident of fate not blood.

"I'm not asking him to wait, Mother."

"He's in love with you."

Jill smiled. "He's in love with love. Since Robin divorced him, he's been looking for a nice cozy marriage to tumble into. That's not love, Mother. That's loneliness. I told him so tonight." *I should know,* she thought. *I've been there.*

"There are worse reasons for a marriage, Jill."

"And better." She'd never been one to string a man along. "He deserves a woman who really loves him." She sat down on the edge of the bed and kicked off her satin pumps. "What happened to my mother, the hopeless romantic?"

Jill smiled; Agneta, however, felt no obligation to return it. "I want you to be happy. I think Tyler is the right one for you."

In twenty-four hours she'd be back in Nevada; there simply wasn't time to pull any punches. And, maybe, she just didn't want to any longer. "Why, Mother? Why do you think he's the right one for me?"

Agneta shifted position on the chaise. "That should be obvious, darling. He's young and handsome. He's well-connected. He's obviously mad for you—" She hesitated, and Jill jumped right in.

"And he doesn't care if I can't get pregnant again?"

Angry slashes of color flooded her mother's face but Jill made no attempt to soften her words. Sterility was a sore point with both mother and daughter. Agneta had never been able to become pregnant, and her adopted daughter's miscarriage and subsequent infertility had opened old wounds that had never fully healed for either one of them.

When Jill's marriage broke up for reasons that included—but weren't limited to—her inability to have children, Agneta's sorrow was intense.

Just how intense was obvious even now.

"Answer me, Mother," Jill said. "Don't avoid it anymore."

"If you must put it so bluntly, then yes." Agneta looked extremely uncomfortable but Jill still did nothing to ease her mother's way. If Agneta felt a compulsion to push the plight of Tyler Austin, she'd be damned if she would aid and abet. "Men like your father and Tyler are hard to come by. You shouldn't turn away so blithely. Running away from reality isn't the answer."

Jill leaned forward and took her mother's narrow, elegant hand in her own. "Don't you understand, Mother? I'm not running away from anything—I'm running *toward* something."

"Playing piano for a group of ranchers in Nevada? What kind of logic is in that, darling? You have a wonderful life here. You're happy. Why would you turn away?"

Jill met her mother's gaze head-on. "Because I'm *not* happy, Mother. Because I haven't been happy for a very long time and if I don't do something now to change things, I'll regret it for the rest of my life."

Agneta looked at her intently before she spoke. "It's uncanny," she said finally. "In some ways you're more Hank's daughter than I am."

Jill laughed. "Strange, isn't it? I've often felt the same thing."

"I should have known you were unhappy, Jillian. I'm sorry."

"Don't be. How could you know something that I've been doing my best to hide from you."

"And now?"

"I've stopped hiding it from both of us. It's time for me to do what I do best." Music was and had always been her passion, and it was time the two of them were reunited.

Agneta remained unconvinced. "Hank's not forcing you into this?"

"He showed me the road, Mother, but I'm the one who chose to take it."

"You realize I don't understand you any more than I understand him?"

"You love me. That's more than enough."

"So you're determined to go through with this—this craziness?"

"Afraid so. Pa's plane comes in tomorrow afternoon to take me back to Nevada."

"I can't appeal to your sense of family honor?"

"Not this time. Besides, Pa's my family, too, and he's all for it."

"There's a world of difference between Hank Wiley and the Von Erons."

"I know." That was one of the reasons Jill was heading west.

Suddenly Agneta brightened. "I could always set up more engagements for you right here in Palm. There's the Hospital Guild and the Pinafore Yacht Club and—"

"Thanks, but no, thanks. They'd be doing it only as a favor for you."

Agneta's brow furrowed. "You're a marvelous pianist, darling. They'd love to hear you play."

"They'd love Muzak if it came with a vodka collins. I'm going where live music is appreciated."

"How can you be sure they'll appreciate you out there? I've lived there, darling. It may not be exactly what you expect."

"And if it isn't, I'll think of something else to do. Mother, my mind's made up. If I'm not going to have a home and a family of my own, it's high time I made something of my life."

"I can't convince you to at least think about it? To at least speak with Tyler about your plans?"

"I've already spoken with Tyler." She'd told him while they were on the dance floor earlier that evening, and he'd stared at her as if she'd said she was descended from the Mayflower Madam. "He's not terribly happy."

"He won't wait for you forever, darling."

"And that's just fine," Jill countered. "I'm going to do this, Mother, no matter who doesn't like it."

"Is there someone else in your life? Is that why you're finding it so easy to dismiss Tyler, a man who has stood beside you for so long?"

Out of nowhere, Tony Graham popped into her head, the way he'd looked the other night at Caesar's Palace, all cocky and confident and more good-looking than perhaps was wise.

Tyler Austin, with whom she had danced less than an hour ago, was a distant memory.

It wasn't something she wanted to try to explain to her very proper mother.

She wasn't entirely sure she could explain it to herself.

"It's the sameness, Mother," she said at last. "I feel as if I'm drowning in sameness." She waved her hand in the air. "The same families, the same schools, the same ways of thinking and feeling and being. I'm not like anyone here and it's time I finally faced that fact."

A glimmer of fear broke through her mother's flawless facade. "Darling, we adopted you from a fine family. We've never done anything but love you because you are our own. Please don't—"

"It has nothing to do with being adopted, Mother. It's everything. I just want more than the life you and Daddy know. I need more." She had no lover, no husband, no child to care for. Shopping and lunching could never fill all the dark and empty corners of her life.

"Be careful out there, Jillian," Agneta said, all pretense of trying to convince her otherwise gone. "You know this world, this way of living. The rules are different. I'd hate for you to do something you might regret."

Jill chuckled but a thread of uneasiness poked through. "Regret? You make it sound as if I were heading out for an extended singles weekend with a wardrobe from Frederick's of Hollywood."

"Western men are different, Jill. Make no mistake about it."

"I'll be careful. Besides, I'll be traveling with a driver, and Pa will be within shouting distance."

"I'll still worry," Agneta said fiercely. "Nothing's going to change that."

"Good," Jill said, hugging the beautiful paradox that was Agneta Von Eron. "That's exactly what a mother is supposed to do."

After Agneta floated off to join guests for drinks in the library, Jill found it hard to settle down. She got out of her gown, pulled her hair back in a ponytail, creamed off her makeup and slipped into her favorite robe. The latest copy of *People* magazine waited on her antique nightstand, but even the lure of learning the latest on Sean and Madonna wasn't enough to capture her full attention. The talk with her mother had crystallized everything she'd been feeling, all of the uncertainties and fears had vanished in front of the undeniable logic of the plan. Hank's idea was the best thing that could have happened to her—and it had come about at the best possible time.

She'd finally adjusted to the realities of her body, to the irregular periods and the apparently irreversible fact that she would never have a child. Oh, Dr. Beauman hadn't ruled it out entirely, but that look in his eyes after he examined her told her all she needed to know.

"First things first," he'd said the last time, trying to tease her out of her sudden black depression. "You need a man before you have a baby, Jill. Elementary biology."

But Jill had had a man—her husband—and nothing had happened, not after that hideous miscarriage.

And she'd mourned the loss of her baby and wept over the end of her marriage and she was ready to put it all behind her and get on with it.

She was ready for change—no, she was hungry for change. She wanted to get out there and try herself in the real world, among people who owed her nothing at all but a chance to entertain them by doing the one thing she knew how to do: play the piano.

She glanced at the clock on her dresser. Five minutes to midnight.

Not quite nine in Nevada.

If she knew Hank, he was probably stretched out in front of his huge stone fireplace with his old mutt, Rusty, on his left and a bottle of Jack Daniels on his right, listening to Patsy Cline records and relaxing after a day of hard work.

She wrapped her arms around her middle and closed her eyes. Central air was no substitute for the clean, cool air of Nevada early spring; Mozart, no match for the crackle of a fire and the soft snore of a sweet old dog.

And, of course, there was her new driver, Tony Graham.

All evening long she'd found herself thinking about him, wondering if Pa were giving him a tough time out there, trying to imagine what it would be like to hit the open road with a man so difficult to predict.

She chuckled softly. Why lie? She was trying to imagine how it would feel to be all alone with a man that attractive.

That magnetic.

That hard to figure out.

The look in his vivid green eyes when they first met had been one of challenge. His whole manner carried such a take-it-or-leave-it attitude of controlled power that she wondered how it was that he'd ended up applying for a job as unimportant as driving her and a baby grand around Nevada.

That evening she'd told Tyler all about her plan, leaning heavily on the trip but dancing lightly over the topic of Tony Graham. Tyler, however, wasn't a stupid man. He caught on instantly to the thrum of excitement building inside her, and neither one of them could pretend it had to do with just playing the piano.

"Whatever it is, be careful," he'd said over the music and the laughter in the ballroom. "I don't want to see you get hurt again."

"I promise," she'd said, kissing his cheek. "Believe me, no one will hurt me again."

But, for the first time, Jill understood exactly what it meant to be the child of two hopeless romantics. There was an undeniable optimism inside her, a certainty that, despite a few false starts, happiness was attainable if she opened herself up to possibilities.

Like getting her act together and taking it on the road to Nevada.

Fifteen hours until Hank's private jet landed at West Palm?

Fifteen hours?

She grabbed the telephone, punched in the area code and number.

"Pa," she said the second the phone stopped ringing, "gas up that old Lear and send it out. I just can't wait any longer!"

Chapter Four

"Who is this?" A man's voice. Definitely not her grandfather's.

"Who is *this*?" she countered. "Where's Hank?" Hank liked to pal around with his buddies, but no one ever wangled an invitation into his log cabin sanctuary—at least, no one with five-o'clock shadow.

"Hank's in the stable. Who the hell is this anyway?"

"His granddaughter. Who the hell are you?"

"His slave."

There was an ironic twist on the word "slave" that keyed her. "Tony?"

"Who else? I get overtime on this job, don't I?"

"I hadn't thought about it." She stretched out on the bed, a foolish grin spreading across her face. "Is Pa working you too hard?"

"Nothing I can't handle, but you could've warned me about the old man—he doesn't know when to quit."

"He has the energy of a kid," she said, then sat up. "You're not having second thoughts, are you?"

"Hell, no. By the time you get here tomorrow night, we'll be just about ready to roll."

"That's why I'm calling. Tell Pa to send the jet out now. I tied up all my loose ends and I'd like to get started."

"Now?"

She laughed. "That's what I said."

He, however, said nothing.

"Speak now, Mr. Graham, or forever hold your peace."

There was a long silence, then: "Ready when you are, Ms. Wiley."

Was she going crazy, or did he sound as if he'd been caught in the middle of a yawn?

"READY WHEN YOU ARE," Tony muttered as he struggled to hang up the phone.

Who was he trying to kid?

Ready for intensive care was more like it.

He hurt in places he hadn't thought about since prep school phys ed classes more years ago than he cared to remember. Outside the window he heard Wiley chopping firewood. Seventy-three years old and in better shape than a man young enough to be his grandson.

Disgusting.

Tony stifled a groan as he slumped down in his chair and positioned the heating pad against the small of his back. Lifting a glass of brandy to his lips took all of his strength while, outside, the old man was whistling while he worked like some demented Disney dwarf.

He'd suggested Tony pick up an ax and join him out there but Tony had muttered an obscenity and retreated to the house in righteous indignation.

Since nine that morning Wiley had worked him harder than Captain Bligh had worked any of the scurvy-ridden deckhands on the *Bounty*. Apologies to

Walt for mixing metaphors but exhaustion did strange things to the mind.

Tony let some brandy slide down his throat—swallowing would have required too much effort.

He rearranged the heating pad and closed his eyes. Visions of forty-ton pianos danced behind his lids.

A helicopter had picked him and Hank up at McCarran Airport and whisked them north to Hank's ranch. Mile after mile of empty land passed beneath his window, punctuated by brush and cactus and an occasional dust storm. How in hell the pilot was able to keep his bearings without landmarks like the Chrysler Building and the World Trade Center had been beyond Tony's comprehension. If it weren't for the odd arrangement of pine trees in the shape of a monogram at the center of Hank's property, they could have been in Nevada or Nepal for all Tony knew.

The helicopter had no sooner touched down when Wiley started cracking the whip.

Who the hell would have figured there would be so damned much involved in driving a woman and a piano around Nevada? No wonder his father had laughed so hard when he called to tell him he had the job and the bet was officially on.

"Good luck," he had said between chuckles. "I think you're going to need it."

The cuckoo clock in the hallway came to life and, if Tony had the energy, he'd have thrown a book at that damned loud-mouthed bird. He didn't need reminding that only twelve hours had passed since he began working for Hank the Hun.

What he did need was sleep. . . .

"Ain't nothin' like hard work to aid the digestion!" A booming voice and a hearty slap on the shoulder. "Oughta try it sometime, boy."

"It's not fair," Tony grumbled, sinking down lower in the chair. "I'm even dreaming about him."

Another slap on the shoulder. "Wake up, Graham. It ain't even ten o'clock yet. Shank of the evening."

"Go away. You're a bad dream."

A huge belly laugh. "The hell I am. Wake up, boy. Who was on the phone?"

Tony yawned and stretched, trying to snap back to the world of the living. "You're a damned slave driver," he said, straightening the collar of his ridiculously out-of-place Lauren polo shirt. "Anybody ever tell you even peons get time off for exhaustion?"

Wiley slapped his knee and laughed some more.

"Glad one of us is enjoying this," Tony said, smothering a smile. "You've been busting my butt all day, Wiley. Don't you ever let up?" Didn't anyone ever tell him he was a senior citizen?

"I'm not lookin' to work you, Graham. I ain't that heartless."

"Could've fooled me."

"None of that wise talk with my Jilly, boy. She'll knock you back on your behind before you can say Jack Robinson."

"Who the hell is Jack Robinson?"

"Don't you young city folk know anything?"

"No," Tony shot back. "We don't know one damned thing, you arrogant old—"

"You got spirit," Wiley said, biting off the end of a cigar and pulling a match out of his back pocket. "You're gonna give my gal a run for her money. I like that."

"I thought I was supposed to play the subservient employee."

"Can the big words, Graham, and say what's on your mind."

This was even better than his weekly poker game cum argument at the Emory Club. "I did can the big words. Not my fault you can't understand me."

Wiley puffed on the big brown cigar. "Don't make that mistake with Jilly. She won't think twice about puttin' you in your place."

"She seems more even-tempered than you, Wiley."

Wiley chuckled, and plumes of smoke curled around his mouth. "Don't you bet on it."

That tiny blonde with the face of an angel—hard to believe she could be more argumentative than this weather-beaten old range warrior in front of him. Tony knew damned well he wouldn't have lasted thirty minutes on the road with Hank Wiley. His granddaughter, Jill, was another story. The thought of thirty days in close proximity to her was—

"Son of a bitch!"

Wiley glared at him. "What did you say?"

"The phone call." He braced himself for another outburst. "Your granddaughter called. She said to send the plane now; she's ready to roll."

Wiley shook his head. "Not a good way to start, Graham. I'm beginnin' to think you just might not work out after all."

Tony groaned and closed his eyes against the vision of a shiny Rolls Royce with his father gloating from behind the wheel. "Wanna bet?"

There were times when a man had to do what a man had to do, and this, it seemed, was one of them.

Antony Graham Wellington IV got up and went outside to chop wood.

IT'S GOING TO HAPPEN, Jill thought as she looked out the kitchen window at the truck parked behind Hank's ranch house. *It's really going to happen.*

From the moment she'd landed in Nevada not quite fourteen hours ago until this second, she'd doubted this whole crazy escapade would ever get off the ground. The Bornsdorfer piano had seemed huge and the brand-new truck—complete with the special suspension system Tony had told her about—seemed too small to ever be able to hold it.

When it came to the truck, Hank and his crew had really outdone themselves. From the outside, it looked like an overgrown horse trailer sans windows—which only served to prove that the old saw about books and their covers still had a lot of merit.

Not only did it house the piano within a temperature- and humidity-controlled environment, it also held an exercise bike, clothes closet, electric piano keyboard for practising and a minirefrigerator.

She sipped her brandy and watched the way the moonlight bounced off the shiny black hood of that incredible truck. She'd spent some wonderful minutes earlier that afternoon watching Tony Graham, shirtless and more muscular than she would have imagined, wielding the Turtle Wax and a chamois cloth under Hank's unforgiving eye.

Her eye had been anything but unforgiving.

She leaned against the sink as a wave of warmth washed over her the way the Nevada sun had earlier, only this time she couldn't blame her heightened temperature on the weather.

She took another sip of brandy and smiled. She couldn't even blame the blessed Benedictine monk who'd fashioned this wonderful liqueur. No, there was but one answer to the strange, unsettling way she had felt that afternoon: biology.

Why had she ever thought herself past those feelings? The last time she'd felt this wonderful tingle of anticipation was back when she and Craig were engaged, and that electric current had fizzled out somewhere between marriage and divorce.

Dancing cheek-to-cheek with Tyler Austin hadn't produced so much as one extra degree of heat; watching Tony Graham wax a truck had turned her midsection into a wood-burning stove like the one crackling in the corner of her grandfather's country kitchen.

The way his back muscles moved beneath his tanned skin, the way the sun splashed gold and auburn in his hair, the way he wiped his forehead with the side of his arm and—

She downed the rest of her brandy in one gulp. She sounded like a love-starved maiden let out of her ivory tower to mingle with the mortals. So what if she found Tony Graham attractive? Plenty of men found her attractive and it didn't mean a thing. What woman wouldn't enjoy looking at a well-built man with his shirt off in the sizzling desert sun?

It didn't mean a thing. It didn't mean spending a month with him in the close confines of the truck would come under any heading other than "business."

It didn't mean it was going to be easy.

Rusty, Hank's old Labrador-shepherd mutt, snored softly at her feet, and she bent down to scratch him behind his left ear.

"Lucky you," she murmured as the sleeping dog instinctively leaned into her caress. "Nothing to worry about except your dreams." The spot behind the dog's ear was velvet soft and warm beneath her fingertips.

Growing up, she'd never had a dog or a cat or even a goldfish—somehow pets didn't seem to be part of the Palm Beach life-style.

Staying at her grandfather's farm had been the equivalent of a trip to Disney World for Jill. And old Rusty had been part of that picture for almost as long as she could remember.

There in that old kitchen with its pine beams and weathered Mexican tiles and wood cabinets with brass fittings that gleamed more beautiful than any jewel she'd ever owned, Jill had learned how to fend for herself. Away from servants and society and the ever-present need to impress, she had discovered the pleasures of solitary pursuit.

After losing her baby, and the nasty divorce that followed, she'd retreated back to Hank's and come to understand one very important thing: Sometimes you had to face what you most feared before you could go on with life.

So, she'd faced the truth of her infertility, taken its full measure and found she was stronger than she'd ever imagined herself to be.

Certainly a month on the road with Tony Graham was something she could handle without undue complications.

"Hi. I saw the light on and thought I'd check."

She looked up and saw her new truck driver standing in the doorway of the kitchen. What was she saying about "undue complications"?

Tony snapped his fingers, and the old dog immediately woke up and, tail wagging, scrambled over to the doorway. Jill couldn't blame Rusty.

Graham looked terrific. His chestnut hair was freshly washed and appealingly rumpled; he wore battered jeans that rode low on his hips, a dark T-shirt and a wide smile.

He was every woman's blue-collar fantasy man: muscles, macho and more male exuberance than should be legal.

"So much for long-term relationships," she said as Rusty fell at his feet in total adoration. "My position has been usurped."

"I wouldn't worry about it," Tony said. "Animals aren't fickle; that's a human characteristic."

She stood up and retied the belt of her silk robe, wondering if she smelled more like dog than Diorissimo. "How long have you been standing in the doorway?"

"Not long." He stepped into the kitchen and let the door swing shut behind him. "Which is it: night owl or early riser?"

"Neither. Insomniac is more like it."

He picked up her brandy glass and sniffed at the remains. "Not bad, but that's not going to do it. You need the strong stuff."

"Not much is stronger than Benedictine." She retreated to the kitchen table where her dishabille might be less noticeable. "If there is, I'm not sure I want to know about it."

He smiled, and even in the semidarkness of the quiet kitchen she knew it was a wonderful smile: all strong white teeth and that hint of a dimple in his left cheek.

"What about warm milk?" he asked.

She made a face. "Disgusting. I hated it when I was a child and I see no reason for an about-face at this late date."

Tony bent down, and his long fingers disappeared into the dog's thick fur as he stroked Rusty's ample belly. The old dog sighed with exaggerated pleasure, and Jill had to remind herself to breathe. She must be more tired than she'd first thought; she could almost feel Tony's hands on her.

"Relax," he said, looking up at her. "I was kidding about the warm milk. What I'm really talking about is exercise."

Dangerous talk for the middle of the night.

"I'm not exactly dressed for running." *Or for anything else you might come up with.*

He slowly unfolded his body, and as he walked toward her, she once again caught the scent of soap and the warmth of the sun.

"I hate running." He flipped a kitchen chair around and straddled it. "I was thinking more like a walk around the south forty. Wiley seems to think this place is Paradise Revisited."

"Pa would shoot you dead if he heard you making fun of his ranch. To him it *is* Paradise."

Tony held his hands up in a gesture of surrender. "I'm not arguing with you. From what I saw, he's got a great spread here. A little bare, but great."

Jill nodded, thinking about the conglomerates her grandfather owned, the land in practically every state in the union and how none of it compared to this scruffy, run-down ranch. "This is his home," she said simply. "The place that matters."

"Do you live here, too?"

"I live in Palm Beach, but I would have sold my best Barbie doll to live here when I was a little girl."

"Palm Beach?"

"Don't sound so surprised. People do live in Palm Beach, you know."

"Rich people live in Palm Beach."

"People of all kinds live in Palm Beach."

He snorted and reached behind him to pull a can of Coke out of the refrigerator. "People with seven-figure incomes live in Palm Beach."

"Do I look like a woman with a seven-figure income?" She was baiting him and she knew it, but having so much fun that she didn't mind risking exposure as a Von Eron.

He made a show of looking her over and, even in the semidarkness, she could feel the way his gaze lingered on the high points of her anatomy. "You don't look like the upstairs maid, Wiley."

"You have something against rich people?"

"It's a long story," he said. "I'll save it for when I know you better."

She pulled out a chair and sat down at the table opposite him. "I wish you'd stop doing that."

He was about to take a swig of Coke and he stopped with the can halfway to his mouth. "Stop doing what?"

"Throwing me a curve. You've been doing it all day. Every time I think I have you figured out, you make a hundred-and-eighty-degree turn."

"Good practice," he said, gulping down some soda. "Wait'll you see me behind the wheel."

"I'm serious," she said, leaning forward. "First you show up for the interview in a Lauren polo shirt and a Rolex—"

"Knockoff," he broke in. "A Rolex knockoff." He wiped his mouth with the back of his hand. "You said so yourself."

"I know I did," she said, wishing she had another brandy but too lazy to get up. "Now I'm not so sure. There's something about you that I just can't figure out."

"Charm? Wit? My incredible body?"

She dismissed his suggestions with a wave of her hand, although the last one did give her a moment's pause. "It's your manner. I just don't have the feeling you really need this job."

"I need it," he said, polishing off the rest of the Coke. "That's one thing you can believe." He looked over at her and grinned. "What makes you think I don't?"

Her silk robe felt sensuous against her skin as she shrugged. "Forgetting the Rolex?"

"Forgetting the Rolex."

"Attitude," she said slowly, trying to put a gut-level hunch into words. "You don't seem comfortable taking orders."

"I'm not," he shot back without missing a beat. "I owned a company, remember?"

She flashed back to their first meeting in Hank's office a few days ago and the story he'd told about a trucking company that went bankrupt. "You're used to giving orders, aren't you?"

"So are you."

"We might have a problem here."

That mercurial smile of his was back. "You're the boss. You give the orders. I follow them."

"It won't bother you, taking orders from a woman?"

"I'm an equal opportunity employee. Taking orders from anyone bothers the hell out of me."

"You're honest, at least."

His smile flickered. "Sometimes."

Another gut-level alarm went off inside her. There was more to Tony Graham than the pat story about the trucking company gone bust, and if she had any sense left to her at this late hour, she'd know that this was the perfect opportunity to call a halt to this whole crazy idea before it went any further. She could give Tony Graham two weeks pay and send him back to New York, then call the hirsute Clarence O'Day and tell him the job was his.

"You look like you're having second thoughts."

She met his eyes. "You read minds, too?"

"It wasn't hard. You were scowling at me."

"Fatigue," she hedged. "Some people yawn; I scowl. It's a family trait."

He looked up at the clock over the sink. "We hit the road in less than ten hours. If you're going to fire me, I'd appreciate it if you'd do it before we leave civilization."

Across the kitchen Rusty grumbled softly in his sleep, and she remembered the tenderness he'd shown the old dog.

"I'm not going to fire you, Tony. Like it or not, the job is still yours."

"I like it." His voice was low and intimate. "I like it just fine."

That same tricky warmth she'd experienced as she watched him wax the truck earlier that afternoon reappeared from nowhere and sent her temperature soaring. She cleared her throat and suppressed an urge to turn on the ceiling fan. "I suppose we should go over a few things before we leave."

He stifled a yawn. "We're going to have a hell of a lot of time to talk once we hit the road, Jill. We should hit the sack."

"We haven't discussed your working hours."

"You're paying me by the job, not the hour. My time is yours."

"I'm not going to need all of it." Her words tumbled out gracelessly. "What I mean is, we'll have plenty of time off to enjoy ourselves."

"Sounds interesting." His expression was bland, but she detected a note of amusement, if not interest.

"What I mean is, we'll have time to enjoy ourselves separately."

"You won't mind if I sample some local color when we're in Branchwater?"

"Of course not." Why was she having difficulty keeping her voice even and her tone neutral? "If you can find local color in Branchwater, feel free to sample it."

"No hard feelings?"

Oh, no, you don't. He wasn't going to turn the tables on her again the way he had during the job interview. "Maybe we could double-date," she said, pushing back her chair and standing up in order to gain the advantage. "I wouldn't mind sampling some local color myself."

Tony Graham might be a truck driver, but he was certainly no fool. Another one of Jill's preconceptions bit the dust as he stood up and eliminated her one advantage. "I thought you were going away on business."

"I am," she snapped, "and my business is none of yours."

He leaned across the kitchen table—all male threat and bluster—but she refused to back down. Who was in charge here, anyway?

It was about time he found out or he'd have one heck of a long walk back from Branchwater.

"Your business *is* my business," he said. "That's why you hired me."

"I hired you to drive a truck, Graham, not play social secretary."

Again that damned twinkle was back in his eye. "Your grandfather told me to look out for you."

"Let's get one thing straight: My grandfather didn't hire you—I did. And I need you to drive, not dictate to me. I had enough of dictators when I was married. I don't need to pay one to do something my ex-husband did for nothing."

"You were married?"

"Yes, and I told you that in Vegas, so don't change the subject. This is a business arrangement, Graham, and it's going to stay that way."

He made a show of looking around the room. "I didn't hear anyone say otherwise, did you?"

"Damn it, you know what I'm talking about. I'm not looking for anything except a driver." *Wrong,* she thought. *All wrong.* She sounded like an outraged maiden trying to convince herself she intended to stay that way.

"And I'm not looking for anything except a job."

Hot color flooded her cheeks as she held his gaze. "Then we shouldn't have any problem, should we? Our cards are all on the table. A simple business arrangement."

He thrust his right hand across the table and clasped hers. "Business arrangement, Ms. Wiley?" His grip tightened. "You got it. I'll drive that truck. I'll move that piano. I'll do any damned thing you want me to, but, lady, when that sun goes down, we're on our own."

His eyes glittered with an emotion she didn't dare identify, and she could literally feel the surge of adrenaline pumping through his body by the way he gripped her hand in his. "Agreed?" he asked.

She matched the pressure of his handshake and increased it a degree. His eyes widened a fraction and inside she glowed in triumph. "Agreed. When the sun goes down, it's every one for himself."

"Or herself?"

"That, too."

He held the handshake a second longer then released her from his grip. "It's going to be a hell of a month, boss lady," he said, grinning. "One hell of a month."

With that he turned and left the kitchen, and she heard him whistling his way up the stairs to his second-story bedroom.

It wasn't until she heard him close his door behind him that she realized he'd been whistling "Take This Job and Shove It."

Chapter Five

"We're not moving." Jill's voice echoed throughout the cab of the world's most expensive horse trailer. "Why aren't we moving?"

Tony turned the key again and heard the depressing grind of the engine refusing to turn over. "We're not moving because the engine won't start."

"Why won't it start?"

"I don't know why," he said, trying to control his temper. "If I knew why, I'd be a mechanic instead of a truck driver."

"You're not a truck driver yet," she pointed out, obviously a woman who liked to live dangerously. "Not if we stay in the driveway all day." She twisted around in her seat and looked in the mirror on her side. "He's still back there. Why don't we ask Pa to take a look?"

Tony glanced in his own mirror just in time to see a huge grin split Hank Wiley's face as he and two of his grizzled old range buddies watched from the back porch of the ranch house.

"The old man probably crossed the wires on me," Tony muttered. "A little ranch humor."

Jill looked at him. "What was that?"

"I said, the wires are probably crossed."

"They weren't crossed an hour ago when Big Al backed it out of the garage."

He glared at her. "Are you always this literal at the crack of dawn?"

She gave him a damnably guileless smile that didn't fool him for a minute. "I'm a morning person, Graham. Rise and shine. Up with the birds. There's nothing like an early start—"

"I'll give you the early start," he broke in, "but don't expect me to like it."

"I'd settle for your being able to start the truck."

She had a point.

He turned the key again and, again, nothing. "Maybe if the old man had put more thought into the engine and less into tooled-leather seats we'd get some place."

"This is a brand-new truck," she said. "Right off the showroom floor."

"I'll look under the hood," he said, unlocking the door. "Maybe the distributor cap is off."

He climbed out of the cab, and Jill slid over behind the driver's seat.

"What are you doing? If it won't work for me, it won't work for you."

"Let me try it once." She had the same manic twinkle in her eye as that damned grandfather of hers.

He leaned against the side of the truck and folded his arms across his chest. "Go ahead. Give it your best shot." It wasn't going to get her anywhere. He was sure of that.

She fiddled with the mirror, adjusted the seat, then turned the key.

"What did I tell you?" She turned to him as the powerful engine roared to life. "All it took was the right touch and voilà!"

He leaned inside the cab. Everything looked the same. "What did you do? Did you and Wiley collaborate on this?"

She laughed, and he could smell a sweet combination of toothpaste and orange juice on her breath. "You forgot to put in the clutch."

"What?"

"The clutch." She pointed toward the pedal to the left of the brake. "You forgot to put it in."

His face burned with an embarrassment he hadn't felt since the time he was twelve years old and forgot to zip up his pants the day of his confirmation, and his Grandmother Parkhurst fainted into her mimosa during brunch.

"Move over," he said, "and let's get this show on the road."

THE ROAD, AS IT TURNED OUT, was mile after endless mile of brush and sand and blazing sun that made the air-conditioned inside of the truck seem like a hermetically sealed icebox. Wiley had told him to head due north for two hundred seventy-five miles, then follow the landmarks toward Branchwater, their first stop.

What Wiley hadn't told him about was just how hard it was to drive this truck. Tony was used to the fingertip control of his Maserati, a machine tailored for comfort and built for speed. Next to that sleek machine, this truck was a lumbering, wheezing mass of pistons and bolts and drive shafts that had all the grace of a Tyrannosaurus rex in heat.

And it didn't have a damned thing to do with the fact that he hadn't been able to start the engine or that he stalled out three times at a red light outside Silver Spur.

He had to hand it to Jill, however. She didn't laugh or try to rub it in. The only thing that gave away her amusement was the telltale twinkle in her eyes, and now that she'd put on sunglasses, he couldn't even see that.

The first hour they kept up a desultory conversation. She chatted about the ranch and old landmarks and some of the geezers who'd been watching their departure. He hadn't talked much; he'd had the feeling Jill was trying to give him a wide berth in deference to his antimorning preference and, after a while, the conversation faded.

She busied herself flipping through her music, humming small snatches of something that sounded vaguely like Mozart.

A leather-bound book was open on her lap, and she scribbled an occasional line in it, alternating between the book and itinerary sheets.

She'd gnawed the eraser off a Number 2 pencil and was doing her best to mangle an innocent Bic Clic when he finally realized what was going on.

He eased the truck around a hairpin curve and was congratulating himself on the maneuver when he saw the look on her face. "What's wrong?" He gestured toward the speedometer. "I'm doing the speed limit."

"I know you are." Her voice was impossible to read, and with those sunglasses on, so were her eyes.

"Then what's the problem?"

She pushed the glasses on top of her head, and he was quick to note the sparkle in her eyes had faded. "You're not going to like it, Tony."

Why should this be any different? So far he hadn't liked anything since he climbed into the truck that morning. He downshifted as they began to climb a hill. "Try me."

"You're going the wrong way."

"The old man said to go north."

She still hadn't taken her eyes off him. "I know."

"So what's the problem?"

"You're going south."

His head jerked in her direction. "The hell I am."

She grabbed the wheel to steady it. "Watch the road, Graham."

He redirected his attention. "I followed his directions to the letter. Make a right, second left, head—"

"North. You didn't."

Normally he would have laughed and told her to stuff it—in the nicest possible way, of course. The incident with the clutch, however, had undermined his confidence. He decided to opt for the logical approach. "You're telling me we're driving south?" His tone of voice made it perfectly clear what he thought of her sense of direction.

"You heard me, Graham. That's exactly what I'm telling you."

"What are you, a Palm Beach Girl Guide?"

"No," she snapped. "Just a woman with a better sense of direction than you have."

"You hired me to drive. Why don't you let me do it?"

"Your driving is fine, but it would be a lot more effective if we were heading in the right direction."

"Why don't you go back to what you were doing and let me worry about it?"

She tossed her Bic down on the dashboard where it immediately slipped into an air vent and started rattling around. "Why should I bother reviewing my music? If we keep going in this direction, I won't have to worry about playing Branchwater tonight."

He tightened his grip on the steering wheel and tried to ignore the incessant click of the pen inside the vent. "You'll be playing Branchwater tonight."

"Do me a favor," she said. "Pull into the next gas station and ask directions. Just to be sure."

He said nothing. A Shell station loomed in the distance and the level of tension in the truck intensified palpably.

"Oh, look!" Jill pointed out the window as they approached the gas station—as if she'd just noticed it that minute. "A station! We could pull in and—"

He left it in the dust. It was becoming a matter of pride. "I'll pull into the next one."

"What if there isn't a next one? This isn't exactly Interstate 80, in case you haven't noticed."

He swerved to avoid a jackrabbit. "I noticed."

"It might be miles before we see another gas station."

"We still have half a tank."

"Damn it! You know I'm not talking about filling the gas tank. I'm talking about getting directions."

She was half facing her window but he caught a good enough glimpse of her face to recognize the set of her jaw as being much the same as the set of old man Wiley's.

Fred's Fill 'Er Up whizzed by.

"You did it again!" Jill's voice was filled with outrage. "You just passed another gas station."

"I told you there'd be another one."

"You also told me you were going to stop."

"We're making great time," he said, glancing away from the road for a moment. "Let's get a few more miles under our belt before we stop."

"My God," Jill mumbled. "You are the most stubborn man on earth."

"You're forgetting your grandfather," Tony said, grinning. "He's got that slot all tied up."

"At least he has a good sense of direction," Jill shot back. "Which is more than I can say for you."

"And you say I'm stubborn? You have a one-track mind."

"You should be so lucky. At least then we'd be heading the right way."

She poured herself another iced tea from the huge thermos they'd brought with them and this time she pointedly neglected to ask him if he wanted more.

They drove in silence through Duck Tail and Eagle Rock, towns smaller than their names. The sun was almost directly overhead, and he knew they should have at least seen a sign for Branchwater by now.

"I know it's probably ridiculously optimistic of me to mention this," Jill said as they approached Crowfoot Pass, "but we're coming up on another gas station. I don't suppose you'd contemplate stopping to ask for directions, would you?"

"I don't need any directions," he said through clenched teeth. How the hell could such a beautiful woman be so persistent?

She peered at the gas gauge. "You could use a little high-test, though."

"We have a quarter tank. We'll be at Branchwater before we're anywhere near empty."

She muttered something under her breath that he didn't catch but he had a strong enough sense of self-preservation to refrain from asking for a repeat.

The Long Island Expressway didn't have as many gas stations as this one-lane road heading nowhere. They zoomed past Gas'n'Go, and Jill's sigh of disgust filled the truck.

A month of this? He must be crazy.

If he had any brains at all, he'd give her her wish and pull over, hand her the keys to the truck and say so long.

Then he'd see how good Hank Wiley's granddaughter was at finding her way around this barren, desolate, godforsaken Nevada desert that sprouted gas stations the way Vermont sprouted maple trees.

He must have been totally out of his mind to have taken this idiotic stunt as far as he had.

A bet was a bet, but he was taking it as seriously as Sloane-Thompson and Brewer and the rest of his father's Emory Club pals took the weekly poker game.

And his opinion of their weekly poker game was what had gotten him into this in the first place.

He didn't need his father to buy him that 1932 Rolls. He didn't need anyone to buy him anything, for that matter. All he needed to do was flash his pedigree and whip out his checkbook and he could have a fleet of cars—or a stable of 747s—if he wanted them.

Thoughts of Emily in London and Rafaela in New York drifted through his mind. He didn't have to be here. All he had to do was—

"Stop this damned car!" Jill's scream exploded into his daydreams.

His foot automatically slammed down onto the brake pedal, and the truck screamed to a skidding, shrieking stop in front of Al's Auto Alley.

"What the hell is the matter?" He scanned the road but saw neither man nor beast blocking the way.

"I wanted you to stop the car," Jill said, retrieving her sunglasses from the floor by her feet. "I must say, my method worked."

"You fool! We could've been killed."

"Don't exaggerate, Tony." She didn't even look contrite. "We would've hit a cactus," she said, with a shrug. "Big deal."

"Why the hell didn't you just ask me to stop?"

"I've been asking you to stop for almost a hundred miles, Graham."

"Next time save your screaming for an emergency." He dragged his hand through his hair and wished he had a cigarette.

"This was an emergency."

"Don't start with that direction business again."

She put her sunglasses back on but he could still feel the force of her scowl. "I won't." She opened the door of the truck and stormed off toward the ladies' room near the mechanic's bay.

He jumped out of the truck and stormed after her. "You're crazy, lady!" he yelled. "You almost get us killed, and now you won't talk about it."

"I said, it's none of your business!"

Amazing that someone so small could walk so fast. He broke into a run and caught up with her as she rounded the corner of the building.

"You owe me an explanation," he demanded. "What was the emergency?"

"It's personal."

"I want to know."

"Use your imagination," she said, pulling away from him. "That is, if you have one."

"What do you mean, use my imagination? What—"

"Iced tea," she said. "Two quarts of it. Are you satisfied now?"

She headed away from him again.

"You're driving me crazy, lady. Iced tea! How can iced tea—"

She pushed open a heavy metal door and stepped inside. Before he could follow her, she slammed it shut in his face. The word *Women* stared back at him in bold white letters.

For a moment he thought of pushing it open and continuing the argument out of the merciless noon sun but if what he'd just seen were any indication, that woman had a temper to be respected.

She did have a point about the iced tea, however.

He turned and was about to search out the men's room when he heard footsteps crunching their way toward him. Just what he needed. Another cigar-chomping, gun-toting, half-baked cowboy who thinks he knows everything there is to know about the world—bound and determined to teach a city slicker a lesson.

"Hi."

He squinted into the glare. That voice sure didn't sound like it belonged to any cowboy he'd ever heard.

A flutter of jasmine floated through the heat and wrapped itself around his olfactory senses.

"You and your wife have a fight?"

"We had a fight, all right, but she's not my wife." *Thank God.* He flipped down his shades and grinned. That silky voice belonged to a woman—well, a girl—who filled out her faded cutoffs and tank top in a very interesting fashion.

"I see." The girl stepped closer. "You need anything?"

"Now, that's a loaded question."

"You sound different," the girl said. "You're not from around here, are you?"

"New York."

She whistled. "What brings you out this way?"

"It's a long story," he said. "You'd never believe it."

"I believe most anything," she said. "It's my worst flaw."

"Fill the tank and check the oil," he said as they headed toward the truck, "and maybe I'll tell you all about it."

And maybe, if he were lucky, she'd tell him Branchwater was right up the road.

"WIMP."

Jill's voice echoed in the tiny bathroom as she examined her reflection in the scratched and spotted mirror. She didn't like what she saw. Not one bit.

She brushed her hair back and scooped it up off her neck with a hot pink banana clip then splashed her face with cool water.

What a sniveling, sorry excuse for a Wiley she was.

"Spineless jellyfish."

That was more like it.

Whose truck was it, anyway?

Judging by the past few hours, it would have been hard to tell.

The second Tony Graham got behind the wheel, he turned into a dictator.

And the second she had climbed into the passenger seat, she turned into the worst kind of wimp imaginable.

Ridiculous as it sounded, she—Jill Von Eron, an intelligent twenty-six-year-old woman—had let that truck driver—her employee—drive one hundred miles in the wrong direction rather than risk a clash with the well-publicized male ego.

Tony Graham might be crazy, but she was a total fool to not reach back and whip out a shiny new Rand McNally map and get them headed in the right direction.

At least she could blame his craziness on testosterone, a product of that wild Y chromosome running amok in his body.

What was her excuse?

Hank would say it was her inbred sense of Palm Beach propriety, the same propriety that had once kept her home writing thank-you notes while her new husband spent time with his polo-playing cronies.

Hank was probably right.

She was paying Tony Graham good money to sit behind the wheel of that truck and drive.

Where he drove was up to her, and she was going to make darn sure he knew exactly which one of them was in control.

She looked into the mirror and saw the reflection of the thousands of pioneer women who'd thirsted their ways across the prairies of this great country because their menfolk were too damned stubborn to stop at the general store to make sure they were heading for Dodge City and not Delaware.

She owed it to womankind to put an end to male tyranny.

"Graham," she said as the rest room door slammed shut behind her, "make my day."

An old cowboy leaning against a battered Coke machine tilted the brim of his hat up and looked at her.

Jill stopped in front of him.

"Can I ask you a question?"

He turned and spat tobacco juice into a bucket a few feet away. "Yep."

"How far to Branchwater?"

He rubbed his chin. "Branchwater? I reckon you got a long way to go, little lady."

She was so happy to hear it that she ignored the "little lady."

She had Graham dead-to-rights. As soon as she got back to the truck, she'd whip out the map and stick the evidence right under his nose.

She'd—

Jill stopped short a few feet from the truck and stared at the tableau before her.

Tony Graham was leaning against the fender, looking altogether too happy for her taste. The reason for his huge smile was lounging against the gas pump, gazing up at him in open lust.

"I'm the boss," she muttered as she walked over toward them. "I'm the boss.... I'm the boss.... I'm..."

She glanced at the girl, who was lucky if she was old enough to vote, then focused her attention on him. "Ready?"

He folded his arms across his chest and met her glare head-on. "Not yet."

"I beg your pardon?"

He motioned toward his nymphet friend. "You owe Taffy $22.25."

"What?"

"Twenty-five gallons of gas at eight-nine per." He grinned at the young girl with the high-test body. "I told Taffy you were good for it."

Jill's eyes darted to the gas pump.

"Don't trust my arithmetic?" he asked.

"If it's anything like your sense of direction, my expense account is in dire trouble."

Taffy's round blue eyes bounced between Tony and Jill like a tennis ball at the U. S. Open.

"You still owe Taffy $22.25," Graham said.

Taffy looked like she'd sacrifice the twenty-two-and-a-quarter if she could keep Tony there a while longer. At the moment, that didn't seem a bad rate of exchange.

Jill pulled out her platinum American Express card.

Taffy shook her head. "Sorry, ma'am. We don't take that."

Ma'am? Jill didn't dare look at Graham. One smirk and he'd have to hitchhike back to civilization.

"Visa?"

Taffy's blond mane swung as she shook her head.

"Mastercard?"

"Un-uh."

"What about cash?" *Last chance, Taffy. Take it or leave it.*

"Yeah," the girl said. "But we don't make change."

Jill fumbled through her wallet and pulled out a twenty and three singles. "Keep the change," she muttered as Taffy stashed the bills in the remarkable valley between her breasts. Another woman might have stashed the money in her bra but Taffy, of course, wasn't wearing one.

Taffy was giving Graham a few unmistakable lessons in body language and, rather than be witness to a grown man's downfall, Jill climbed into the truck and had the road atlas out and the way to Branchwater highlighted by the time Graham got his seat belt adjusted.

"I already know," he said, starting up the engine. "Taffy gave me directions to Branchwater."

She counted to ten before she trusted her voice. "With apologies to your friend Taffy, I'd rather rely on the map."

"We're three hundred and ten miles south of Branchwater. We have to retrace our steps."

"We wouldn't have to retrace our steps if you'd listened to me in the first place."

"Do you want to sit here the rest of the day talking about Branchwater, or do you want to get there in time for your show?"

She glanced at her watch and saw it was a little after noon. The show was at eight, and unless Graham shifted from neutral straight into warp three, it was going to be a close call.

Her dreams of a long, hot bath and an hour's practice vanished, thanks to his male ego and her female stupidity.

She'd be lucky if she got there in time for the curtain.

"I think it's time we got a few things straight," she said, pushing the map toward him. "I'm the boss; you're the employee. I pay for the gas; you flirt with the pump jockey. I tell you where we're going; you drive us there. And you can take that damned Y chromosome and stick it in your ear. Got it?"

He looked at the road atlas for so long that Jill wondered if he'd somehow managed to daydream during her entire speech.

"Did you hear me?" she asked, gearing herself up to repeat it—more forcefully, this time.

He rested the map on the console between them then executed a perfect military salute. "Loud and clear, boss." He threw the truck into gear and roared out of the gas station, leaving the beauteous Taffy behind to contemplate the vagaries of fate.

"You don't have anything more to say?" Jill asked.

"Nope."

"No explanations? No defense?" *No apologies?*

"You've said it all, Ms. Wiley." He hung a sharp right that had her grabbing the armrest to steady herself. "You're the boss; I'm the employee. You pay for the gas; I flirt with the sexy redhead. I—"

"I didn't say that. I never said anything about a sexy redhead." She'd hated redheads ever since her ex-husband left her to marry one.

He didn't miss a beat. "—drive; you tell me where to go. I—"

"Enough!" In her entire life, Jill had never screamed at another living soul and now, in the space of a few hours, she'd exercised her vocal cords twice—and at the same person. Thank God she wasn't a concert soprano. "You're not my husband, Graham. You're not my boyfriend, you're not my brother. I don't have to make allowances for your damnable male pride. This is a business arrangement, and if that doesn't suit you, you can go out and find another arrangement that does. I'm sure Taffy would have a few suggestions."

"She probably would," he snapped. "But I'm not fool enough to take her up on any of them."

So he had noticed she was a lot younger than her measurements would indicate. Score one for him.

"I'll repeat what I said before: This is business, Graham, not a battle of the sexes. If you can't work for a woman, say so now and we'll part friends." *Or at least we'll part alive.*

A small muscle near the base of his jaw clenched, and she braced for an explosion.

"Are you finished?" he asked, his voice deadly even.

Her righteous indignation faltered. "Yes. Quite finished."

"Great." He turned his head for a moment to look at her, and she resisted the impulse to grab the steering wheel. "Now it's my turn."

"Yes?"

"As you said, I'm paid to drive." He directed his full attention back to the road, and she exhaled softly in relief. "I'll let you know when we get there."

And those were the last words he uttered.

Which, at the moment, was their first step in the right direction: north.

To Branchwater.

Chapter Six

After six hours and forty-nine minutes of silence, Tony finally spoke.

"About five miles more," he said, sounding a lot like Jason from *Friday the 13th*.

Of course, the creaking, rusty sound of his voice shouldn't have surprised him. This was the longest he'd ever gone without speaking since he'd first mastered the art.

The first hour of his self-imposed silence had been easy. He was still nursing a healthy anger over Jill's sudden decision to exercise her authority. The second hour was almost over by the time he realized she was napping. Along about the third hour he'd figured she'd be asking him to pull over into a rest area any moment and this gathering silence would finally be broken—and she'd be the one to break it.

She didn't.

Four hours passed.

Then five.

Then six.

The silence deepened until it felt like a third presence in the cab of the truck. He'd never known a woman as stubborn before. He'd been ready to call a truce about the time they whizzed through Snake Flats. Counting cacti had lost its charm about fifty miles out of the gas station. He wasn't a man used to communing with nature or delving deep into his own psyche for entertainment.

A little conversation would have been nice right about then.

But it was pretty obvious that Jill Wiley had decided that he was a degree or two beneath the rest of humanity. As she'd said, he was an employee—and a pretty menial one at that—and had put him in his place.

And that place to which she'd relegated him wasn't anywhere Antony Graham Wellington IV had ever been before.

Jill had been right when she said he was used to giving orders. He hadn't realized just how right until the helicopter dropped him off at Hank's ranch and his life as a wage slave began.

The old man had worked his tail off but at least he didn't give a damn if Tony shot his mouth off—something he did frequently as the day on the ranch wore on.

That, however, was poor preparation for working for his granddaughter. Compared to her, Hank Wiley was Mother Teresa.

Jill Wiley was tougher than an army drill sergeant—not that he knew anything about drill sergeants except what he'd seen in movies but, all things considered, it seemed an apt analogy.

Last night she'd been warm and witty, and again he'd felt the stirrings of attraction building inside him as he enjoyed the way her blond hair tumbled over her slender shoulders and imagined how she'd feel in his arms.

Today she was a different woman. Tense, short-tempered, given to spurts of good humor followed quickly by a display of whip cracking that made him wonder if it all was worth it.

Was this the way ninety percent of Americans dealt with every day of their working lives? Worrying about the arbitrary moods of a boss who held a family's future in his or her hands? For Tony it wasn't even a matter of financial life and death, and he still felt as if he were walking a tightrope with a shark tank below and a starving lion at each end.

Balancing personal integrity and independence with the attitude of compliance demanded by the workplace was a Gordian knot. He couldn't imagine what it would be like to have the added burden of economic necessity.

What the hell was he doing pretending to understand what it was like to actually *need* a job? What the hell was he doing pretending this was actually going to pan out?

There was no way he and Jill Wiley were going to make it through thirty days. Hell—it was a good thing Branchwater was right up ahead because he doubted they'd last another thirty minutes.

He was too independent, too aware of his own place in society to take orders from anyone. If he'd learned anything today, he'd learned that. Every suggestion she made, every wisecrack she uttered, got inside his gut and made him burn with indignation.

He wasn't cut out for this.

He'd see her through the show tonight and get her back to Hank's tomorrow.

And, after that, she was on her own.

He'd walked away from a lot of things in his life. What was one more?

Branchwater made Silver Spur, Hank's home town, look like Manhattan on the last shopping day before Christmas. As Graham drove down what passed for Main Street, Jill counted two stop signs, three five-and-dimes, and one bank that also doubled as the post office.

A woman in a pale blue shirtwaist dress and tan blazer was locking the door of the Branchwater Insurance Company for the night and she turned and stared as the truck rolled by.

"There's no one around," Jill said, forgetting the almost seven hours of hellish silence they'd just endured. "What has Pa gotten me into?"

Tony Graham glanced at the digital clock on the dashboard. "It's 6:14," he said. "They're probably all having dinner."

"Yes," she said, dread flooding her body. "All six of them."

He smiled briefly, and they continued to the northern edge of town where Hank had reserved two rooms for them at a place called Bea's, which was supposed to be right across from the Masonic Lodge where she'd be playing tonight.

Tony made a left turn into a gravel driveway and stopped the truck.

"Last stop, Branchwater." He shut off the engine and set the emergency brake. "Everybody out."

She looked at the small one-story brick building in front of them and at what appeared to be a Quonset hut with landscaping across the street.

"You are kidding, aren't you?"

"I wouldn't kid you, boss lady. You gave me orders not to." He unfolded a piece of pale brown paper, and she could just make out Hank's sprawling script. "Bea's

Rest Stop," he said, handing the paper to her. "Just in case you don't believe me."

She looked at the paper then at the painted sign over the front door of the motel. "Bea's Rest Stop," it said. "Home to Weary Travelers Since 1952." She leaned across the stick shift and looked out Tony's window. "And that's the Masonic Lodge?"

"You got it."

She slumped back in her seat.

Nothing was going the way she'd planned.

Not the trip.

Not their relationship.

Not this town that seemed too small to populate a phone booth.

A wave of nausea suddenly rose from her feet, and she swallowed hard against it.

Terrific.

Stage fright on top of everything else.

She grabbed her overnight bag and music and hurried into Bea's to register and get ready for the show, leaving Graham to figure out how to get the piano out of the truck and into the lodge across the street.

That was the easy part.

The hard part was convincing herself to join it there later.

"SOMEONE WAXED THE KEYS!" Jill knew her voice was somewhere in the register reserved only for dogs and alien beings but she couldn't help it. "What am I going to do?"

Of course it was a rhetorical question since the show was going to begin in three minutes and, short of a visitation by the goddess of traveling pianists and a gift of another Bornsdorfer, she was in big trouble.

"What on earth made you do it, Tony? Was it your idea of a joke?" She ran her fingers across the keys and groaned. "This is like crossing a skating pond in spike heels."

He took a drag on a cigarette and shook his head. She had to admit he looked nearly as upset as she was. Not that that was any consolation.

"One of the men who helped unload the piano said waxing it before a performance enhances the sound."

Her fingers slid silently over a few chords. It was going to be an unmitigated disaster. "You wax the *wood*," she said, her voice an F-sharp, "not the *keys*."

Tony started to say something but two men from the Masonic Lodge came over to shake her hand.

"We're real pleased to have you here in Branchwater, Miss Wiley," the taller of the two said in a voice best described as booming. "When your granddaddy called and told us about your service, why we jumped at the chance."

"Thank you," Jill said, shaking his hand. "I'm glad you did."

"Don't get too much live entertainment out this-a way," the shorter man chimed in. "The missus was so excited she poked holes in three pairs of stockings when she was gettin' ready tonight."

She tilted her head and looked at him curiously. "Really?" *For me?* She didn't dare look at Graham. He was probably laughing his head off.

"You bet." The shorter man clapped her on the shoulder. "Been a long hard winter here, miss. You're like a breath of spring comin' through."

An odd warmth suddenly blossomed inside her chest, and her stage fright cracked and broke apart like a block of ice beneath a sledgehammer.

"Two minutes!" called the woman from the insurance company who also doubled as stage manager.

Jill flashed her a thumbs-up sign. Adrenaline sang through her body like the "Hallelujah Chorus." The two men hurried away to claim their folding chairs on the other side of the makeshift curtain.

Laughter and conversation floated toward Jill and for the first time since they left Hank's that morning, she was glad to be where she was.

"One minute, Miss Wiley."

She ran through her finger exercises, took a deep breath, then caught Tony's eye.

They looked at each other for a moment, and she was about to glance away when an unexpected smile flickered across his face. Just as the curtain began to open, the words "Break a leg!" proved that the acoustics of the Masonic Lodge in Branchwater, Nevada, weren't bad at all.

Carnegie Hall, she thought as the applause rushed toward her, *eat your heart out.*

THE CONCERT WAS A DISASTER.

From the moment her fingers slid right past middle C in her opening number to the second her last selection was halted by a chorus of crying children in the front row, it was obvious to Tony that Jill Wiley was fighting a losing battle.

For two hours he'd watched as she struggled against fatigue, an out-of-tune piano and an audience whose enthusiasm began to wane after the third Chopin variation.

And, to his intense surprise, for two hours he'd found himself struggling along with her. By the time she stood up and took her bows, Tony was drenched in sweat.

What in hell was the matter with him? He'd endured almost eight hours of deadly silence in that truck with her that afternoon, and his anger had escalated so that just the sound of her breathing got under his skin.

Why then had he stood there throughout her whole damned program? He could have been relaxing over a huge steak instead of wasting his time watching his soon-to-be ex-boss waste hers.

The only thing that had gotten her through the concert was the sheer strength of her will.

He would have quit the second he realized the piano was grossly out of tune.

He would have pitched a major fit when the lighting flickered then died.

The cigarette smoke, the shrieking babies, the total lack of professionalism would have sent him raging out of there, ready to head back to Palm Beach or wherever the hell it was she came from.

Not Jill.

She sat there on that piano bench and she played her heart out.

Piano techniques learned at Juilliard and the Mozarteum were showered on the residents of Branchwater, Nevada. Population: 987.

She never let on that she knew she wasn't in Carnegie Hall, that those sixty-watt bulbs overhead weren't klieg lights, that the ranchers and schoolteachers and children weren't part of the glitterati.

No, she gave them everything she had.

Wholeheartedly.

Without reservation.

The way he'd never done one damned thing in his entire life except have a good time.

When it was over she stayed on for a while, talking to the insurance saleswoman/stage manager, a few young couples with small children in tow and the members of the Methodist Sewing Circle who'd attended en masse. What was amazing was the way she behaved as if the past two hours had been a resounding success.

It wasn't until the Branchwater Police and Fire Department—which consisted of a man named Freddy, his son Eddy and their cousins Teddy and Arnold—rolled up their collective sleeves and pitched in to help load the piano back on the truck that her guard slipped and he saw fatigue and a touch of vulnerability on her lovely face.

"You okay?" he asked, walking Jill outside.

"Fine. Just tired." She took a deep breath of early spring air. "Do you have enough help with the piano?" Unloading it had been almost as disastrous as the show itself.

"I have the entire police and fire departments this time. Who could ask for more?"

She nodded and turned to leave.

"Jill!" He caught her by the sleeve of her white silk shirt. "Are you sure you're okay?"

She stepped off the curb, neatly moving out of his reach. "I'm fine. Postperformance blues." She started across the street.

He shoved the sleeves of his workshirt up over his forearms. Why not? he thought. There was never going to be a good time to tell her he was bailing out. He might as well—

"Tony!" Big Freddy Watson hollered from the doorway of the lodge. "Back the truck around. We got 'er ready to go."

He hesitated in the middle of the street and watched as Jill disappeared up the driveway of Bea's Rest Stop.

He'd tell her later, he thought as he climbed into the truck and gunned the engine.

One thing was sure: In a town this size she shouldn't be hard to find.

AN HOUR LATER the piano was bolted into its special suspension cradle and the truck was locked tight, something that Freddy, the chief of police, seemed to find pretty funny.

"Don't need locks in Branchwater," he said as Tony pocketed the keys. "Don't have no burglars."

Tony chuckled. "So what do they need you and the guys for, Freddy?"

"Beats the heck out of me, young fella. Been tryin' to figure that one out since 1953."

Teddy and Eddy, with Arnold bringing up the rear, joined them in the driveway of the lodge.

"We're goin' to have a few Coors over at Arnold's," Teddy said. "You want to join us? We'd be real pleased."

"I wish I could," Tony said, surprised to discover that he meant it, "but I better go see how the boss is doing."

They nodded, all men who understood about work and bosses and the things that made up daily life.

"Been real nice," said Freddy, pumping Tony's hand up and down. "Real nice."

An idiotic lump formed in Tony's throat as he shook the others' hands in turn.

"Maybe we'll see you again," said Arnold. "Tell the lady she just about made our day."

"I'll tell her," he said. "You can bet on that."

Jill wasn't in her room when he got back to Bea's—either that or she wasn't answering her phone. Maybe she was soaking in a warm bath with a cloud of bubbles just barely covering her—

"Forget it," he said, startling the young room clerk who lounged behind the desk watching a tiny color TV.

"Sir?"

"Sorry." Tony forced some incredible images from his mind. "Just talking out loud." His stomach rumbled alarmingly, and it struck him he hadn't eaten since that morning. "Any place I can get something to eat around here?"

The desk clerk looked up at him as if he'd asked for a magnum of Taittinger's and a crock of pâté to go.

"You want something to eat?"

"That's the general idea. Is any place open?"

"Well, the Pancake Palace might be."

"Sounds great." A stack of blueberry pancakes to fortify him for breaking the news to Jill wasn't a bad idea. "Can I walk there?"

The desk clerk laughed. "Pancake Palace is in Reeve Junction."

"Which is where?"

"Thirty miles north."

"Anything closer?"

The clerk looked at the clock on the wall behind him. "Not at this hour." He gestured toward the hallway. "Got some vending machines out that way if you're interested."

His stomach growled again. "I'm interested." He fished some singles out of his pocket and tossed them on the desk top. "Quarters," he said. "Lots of them."

A few minutes later he'd relieved the vending machines of four Milky Ways, two Hershey bars and three lukewarm cans of Pepsi and was on his way back to his room for a chocoholic's feast.

His room was on the second floor, accessible only by a rickety wooden staircase out back. He rounded the building and was headed past the swimming pool when he caught sight of someone sitting in the shadows near the missing diving board.

"Jill?" he called out. It had to be. Everyone else in Branchwater was asleep. "Is that you?"

The shadowy figure moved back into the darkness as he approached, his arms filled with caloric bounty.

"Yes," she said finally, her voice muffled and husky. "I thought you'd be asleep by now."

He stopped about ten feet away from her but the shadows still hid her from view. "Unfortunately I can't sleep on an empty stomach."

She groaned. "Don't mention dinner. There's nowhere open for at least a forty-mile radius."

"Thirty," he said, "but who's counting?" He tossed two Milky Ways into her lap and sat down next to her on a redwood bench. "Join me? My boss gave me an expense account."

"Don't start a fight now," she said. "I don't have the energy for it."

"I don't expect you to believe this, given past experience, but I was trying to make you laugh."

"I'm too tired to laugh."

"Come on." He waved a Hershey bar in front of her nose. "I know it's not prime rib but it beats starvation."

"I suppose so." She ripped off the paper and took a bite. "Thanks, Graham. This is the highlight of my day."

She turned to look at him at last, and he was struck by how small she was. In the moonlight her hair glimmered a pale blond, framing a face of such delicate proportions that he was hard put to equate this ethereal creature with the slave driver he'd worked with earlier in the day.

It was almost enough to make him reconsider quitting his job.

Almost, but not quite.

He gobbled a Milky Way for strength.

"Jill," he began, "we need to talk."

"I already know what you're going to say."

He tore into an other one. "You do?"

She daintily wiped her hands on the clean side of the candy wrapper and reached for a can of Pepsi resting at the edge of the swimming pool. "Of course I do. I'm not stupid, Tony." She met his eyes, and an odd, jittery feeling began somewhere inside his body. "I was awful. I know that."

She didn't break eye contact, and he didn't dare look away. "You weren't awful," he hedged.

"Semantics. I was terrible, rotten, stinking, horrible— You can stop me anytime, you know."

A grin began to break across his face despite himself. "You haven't hit 'lousy' yet."

She glared at him, and he was actually glad to see she hadn't lost all of her fighting spirit, but the sparkle in her eye was still extinguished.

"Loyalty," she said, taking a gulp of Pepsi. "I love that in an employee."

It was the perfect chance to tell her he was no longer an employee but it slipped past him. Damn, but he missed that sparkle in her eyes.

"It was the piano," he said instead. "We should have had it tuned before the show."

"When? We barely got here in time for the curtain."

"That was my fault." Had he really said that? He, Antony Graham Wellington IV, the man who never apologized for anything? "If I hadn't gotten us lost you would have had plenty of time to take care of all that."

She leaned back against the bench and closed her eyes. How fragile she looked in the silvery splash of moonlight. How beautiful.

"Don't blame yourself, Tony," she said. "Tuning the piano would never have occurred to me. There's always been someone else to take care of the details." Her breasts, outlined by the soft silk blouse, rose and fell with her sigh. "This isn't as easy as I thought it would be."

Tell me about it.

If he could just say the words, by this time tomorrow, he could be back in New York, in his fancy Trump Tower apartment, with a woman more willing—and less complicated—than this gorgeous blond bundle of contradictions.

"Hell," she said, opening her eyes and giving him a sleepy smile, "why not admit it? I haven't had this great a time in years."

He stared at her. "What?"

She pushed her hair off her forehead with a movement so inherently graceful that it kept replaying inside his head. "I know the piano was out of tune and the acoustics were terrible and my fingers slipped on the keys like Dorothy Hamill's skates on wet ice but I *got* to them, Tony. Despite everything, I really got to them."

He didn't know what to say to her. His own view of the evening hadn't extended beyond seeing the show end before the piano lid closed on her fingers.

"What do you mean?" He didn't remember cries of "Encore!" or a standing ovation.

"I thought I'd lost them with the Chopin," she said with surprising candor, "and I was beginning to worry about the Mozart when I looked out at them and saw their faces." She stopped and shook her head in amazement. "They didn't care that I wasn't perfect. They didn't care that the piano wasn't up to par. They didn't walk out when I stumbled in the middle of the Mozart. I've been replaying the whole show in my mind for two hours now, Tony, and I know I was awful but it just didn't matter. They *liked* me, flaws and all."

The sparkle was back in her huge gray eyes, and he felt himself being drawn to her in a way he didn't know how to deal with.

She chatted on about the comments the ranchers and teachers and homemakers had made when the show was over, of the sheer appreciation they'd shown that she would even bother with Branchwater, and he remembered the honest friendliness of the men who helped him move the piano. And, deep down, he knew it wasn't a lack of sophistication on their part that made the difference: It was just that they'd managed to maintain a perspective about what was really important in a way their counterparts back in New York and Palm Beach had not.

Kindness still existed out here.

Friendship mattered.

Making an effort really counted.

Imagine what they would have thought if she'd had a tuned piano.

Talk about a brave new world. . . .

His emotions rushed in at him, emotions so complicated and unexpected that he tried to sidestep them before they got the better of him. Jill Wiley with her sharp tongue and soft beauty was unlike any woman he'd ever known. She carried herself with a fierce independence yet wasn't afraid to let down her guard—usually when he least expected it—and let him glimpse her woman's heart.

If he'd learned anything at all at Yale, he'd learned how to keep moving. He looked at Jill and tried to ignore the way the moonlight laced her hair with silver and turned the twinkle in her eyes to star fire.

He wanted out of this situation, didn't he? He was looking for the easy, graceful exit line that had never failed him before.

"Don't get too sure of yourself," he said gruffly. "This was only your first stop. The next group may not be so enthusiastic."

She looked him straight in the eye. "They will be. I won't give them the chance to be anything but."

"Then you better get that piano tuned at every stop."

She waved her hand airily. "We can arrange something."

We?

"What about the wax on the piano keys?"

"I'll wash them down in the morning. It's not permanent."

"What about if the next crowd hates Mozart and loves the Judds?"

She snapped those long, artistic fingers of hers. "Then I'll play requests. I'm a very versatile woman, Tony."

He was beginning to see that the woman he'd met in her grandfather's office was only one of many Jill Wileys hiding beneath that beautiful—and deceptive—exterior.

She was committed to this project with or without him; of that he was sure. If he turned and walked, she'd still head off for Paiute Hollow tomorrow morning even if she had to push the truck the whole way.

It wasn't for money or for fame, because she sure wasn't going to find either one of them on the back roads of northern Nevada.

And the odds were good she didn't have a Rolls Royce bet going with her grandfather. Tony smiled to himself. He'd already seen the vintage Caddy the old man favored.

The only reason for her being here, the only reason he could come up with, was the pleasure she got from sitting down at that grand piano and doing with her talent what she was meant to do: play her heart out.

If there were a better reason for doing something, he'd never encountered it.

And that's when he knew he'd signed on for the long haul.

"Was there something you wanted, Tony? I was so busy raving about my own performance that I—"

He raised his hand to stop her. "It wasn't anything. Forget it."

There was no way he was going to miss out on this adventure. He gathered the crumpled candy wrappers and empty soda cans and stood up.

"Where are you going?" she asked, stifling a yawn.

"Bed."

She maneuvered his wrist into a narrow ribbon of moonlight so she could read his watch. "So early?"

He hoped his shrug conveyed the requisite degree of studied nonchalance. Her simple touch had made him feel anything but. "Why not? If we're getting an early start for Paiute Hollow, I'd better get some sleep." He backed slightly out of her reach, and her hand fell into her lap. "I'll see you in the morning."

He turned to go back to his room, wondering what Rafaela and his old pals would think if they could see his accommodations at Bea's Rest Stop, when her soft voice halted him in his tracks.

"Tony," she called out just before he rounded the swimming pool.

He stopped and looked back but she was just a shadow in the silvery darkness.

Only her voice was real as she said, "I'm glad you didn't quit."

Her soft laugh followed him up the stairs to his room, and the memory of the way she'd looked in the moonlight stayed with him long after he fell asleep.

JILL WAS CERTAIN she was going mad.

All she had done was touch Tony's wrist so she could see the time. They hadn't kissed or held hands or done any of the things associated with romance, yet she felt as if the moon and stars above had suddenly decided to zero in on Branchwater just for them.

What had happened in the Masonic Lodge had been wonderful: She couldn't deny the sheer joy of playing piano for an audience eager for live music. But the slick feel of the ivory keys couldn't compare to the warmth of Tony's skin and the strong pulse throbbing beneath her fingertips.

And she couldn't help but wonder how that pulse would feel against her lips, against her—

Her laughter bounced off the still waters of the pool.

"Mad," she whispered. She was mad, crazy, wild with desire so intense that even the cool night air couldn't compete with the fever dancing through her.

She glanced over at the staircase to the second floor.

All she had to do was put one foot in front of the other and climb those whitewashed wooden stairs.

All she had to do was knock on the door of Room 205 and let nature take its course.

One night was all she wanted.

One night would be enough.

But somehow she knew one night with Tony Graham wouldn't be enough, couldn't be enough.

And so Jill Wiley sat alone by the pool behind Bea's Rest Stop and thought about how wonderful it would have been in that room on the second floor.

Chapter Seven

From that night on, everything between Jill and the mercurial Tony Graham changed.

And what was really amazing to Jill was the fact that things had changed for the better.

When he found her by the pool behind Bea's Rest Stop for Weary Travelers, she'd known immediately that he was about to toss the truck keys in her lap and bid her a not-so-fond farewell.

The tension that had been between them since they first climbed into the Chevy that morning had been building and building, and she was certain that he'd decided the upscale pay he was getting wasn't worth the decidedly downscale way they'd been getting along.

It was something she understood. How many times that day had she resisted the urge to kick him out along the side of the highway and tell him to hitch his way back to Vegas and civilization?

A woman accepted idiotic behavior from a husband or lover. A woman didn't have to accept idiotic behavior from an employee.

It had taken her a while to figure that one out, but once she had, she didn't hesitate to put her newfound sense of authority into action. The result had been the blowup at Taffy-the-nymphet's gas station and the growing certainty that they'd be parting company at Branchwater.

The only question had been whether he would quit before she had a chance to fire him.

But that night by the pool something had happened. A strange connection between them had been made, something that she couldn't have explained to anyone, much less herself. She could have let him go at any moment. He could have quit any time.

Instead he brought her candy bars and Pepsi for a midnight supper, and she had let him see another part of her heart that few people had ever bothered to discover.

Her love for the piano—that secret, unbridled passion for the miracle of music—was something few people cared about. She wasn't altogether sure Tony Graham understood it, but he seemed to take some pleasure from her own enjoyment and frequently surprised her with cogent observations on her performance and sharp questions about her future plans.

Things she'd never shared with her husband she shared with Tony as the truck covered the miles. Her love of Dickens and English sheepdogs, her passion for piña coladas and Picasso, the way she felt each time an eagle soared overhead—all the private, deeply personal feelings, and the silly ones, as well, tumbled out.

What had started out as open warfare was slowly, amazingly, turning into something approaching a friendship.

And now, nine days after they battled their way to Branchwater, she found herself eager to wake up every morning, eager to see him over breakfast in some little truck stop in the foothills of the Sierra Nevada, eager to spend time with him, talk with him, laugh with him.

He surprised her the morning after her first show with a list of piano tuners who would be eager to help when she came to their towns. He'd even called ahead to make certain her uncommon Bornsdorfer would pose no problems. Volunteer fire departments and high school wrestling teams stood ready to serve as piano movers.

And he told her stories during those long stretches of highway driving—possibly apocryphal but marvelous nonetheless—about his college days, and risqué jokes that made her laugh out loud in a way that would stun her Palm Beach pals.

"You have a great laugh, boss lady," he'd said the other day after telling her a particularly juicy tale about Yale protocol and the toga party that had amazed New Haven and points east.

"That was a great story," she'd said. "Are you sure you're just not giving me the plot of *Animal House*?"

"What would you know about *Animal House*? Somehow I can't imagine it at the Palm Beach Playhouse."

"You're right," she said. "I was sixteen and up at Miss Porter's School and we sneaked into town to see it."

"Shocked you, did it?"

She called upon her best Von Eron look. "Of course it did." She'd struggled to keep another laugh from bursting out. "How would you feel if you discovered you'd been tying your toga on the wrong shoulder?"

He'd looked at her for a full ten seconds before he started to laugh with her.

It seemed to Jill they spent an inordinate amount of time laughing.

She was certain she'd laughed more with Tony Graham in nine days than she had in three years with her ex-husband.

That wasn't something a woman could easily overlook.

Great biceps you could get at Jack LaLanne.

A sense of humor you were born with.

Lucky Tony Graham had both.

The boundaries between them began to crumble with the miles as they ventured into the magnificent wilderness of northern Nevada.

You couldn't spend hour after hour alone with a man under such intimate conditions and maintain those barriers for long.

They'd even begun to take turns driving, with Jill spelling him at the wheel occasionally so he could rest his eyes and snap out of highway hypnosis. Being a permanent passenger was duller than practicing scales, and each time she dozed off in her seat, she woke up with a start, terrified that she'd either snored or fallen asleep with her mouth open and drooled all over her linen camp shirt and he was too smart an employee to mention it.

And so on their tenth morning together, Jill was in the driver's seat, easing the truck around a hairpin curve in the Sierra Nevada while Tony thumbed through *People* magazine and whistled along with a Huey Lewis and the News cassette.

"I wish you'd picked a different road," she said, slowing down over a particularly nasty patch.

He looked out the window, then at her. "So do I. That must be a thousand foot drop out there."

Sweat broke out along her hairline and at the back of her neck. "Maybe you should take the wheel. This looks like a job for a professional."

"You're doing fine, boss lady," he said, adjusting his seat belt. "The road opens up about a quarter mile ahead."

Loose rocks and pieces of asphalt kicked up from the tires and clanked against the frame of the truck. One bounced off the windshield, and she had to call upon all of her self-control to keep from squeezing her eyes shut in self-defense.

"I'll stop here," she said, gripping the wheel. "You can climb over and drive the rest of the way. No hard feelings." At that point she didn't care if he called her a woman driver and asked if she'd bought her license at Neiman-Marcus; all she knew was that she didn't want to drive anymore.

He took another look out the window. "Are you crazy? You stop this thing and we could get rear-ended. Keep going."

She checked her rearview mirror and saw empty road behind her. She'd been seeing empty road behind her for the past two hours. "I think the nearest car is in Colorado," she said through chattering teeth. "You're the professional truck driver. I want you to drive."

"Listen to me, Jill—"

She turned to glance at him.

"Don't *look* at me, for chrissakes!" He reached out to steady the wheel. "I'm going to be blunt with you: The road on my side is crumbling. You have about three inches, four the most, to spare."

One of Hank's earthy ranch-hand curses sprang from her lips.

"Interesting," said Tony. "I wouldn't have thought a pig could. Now listen to me: You can't stop. With that wind blowing through the canyon, the slightest extra movement could tip us over the edge and it's bye-bye Bornsdorfer—not to mention us. Keep the wheel steady, do what I say and I swear to you in about three minutes this will be all over."

"Poor choice of words, Graham," she muttered.

They approached an incline.

"Shift into low," he said. "That will give us better traction."

She did, and the truck fell back for a second then moved forward in surer tracks.

"I have to be crazy," she said. "Root canal is better than this."

"Shut up and concentrate," he snapped. "There are fallen rocks up ahead."

Panic returned full force. "What do I do—go around them?"

"Go over them."

"You're crazy."

"This isn't a multiple choice quiz, Wiley. It's go over the rocks or off the cliff."

"I see your point."

He told her what to do to maintain control. The air conditioning wasn't enough to compensate for fear, and beads of sweat trickled down her forehead and into her eyes. She blinked rapidly to clear them, not daring to take her hands from the wheel.

Tony, thank God, saw her predicament and wiped her brow with a tissue from the glove compartment.

"Just hang on," he said, his voice the one solid thing in her world at that moment. "Just a little more...keep that wheel steady...ease up...that's it...that's it! You did it!''

She sailed into the straightaway where the road split into two lanes, and pulled over onto the shoulder.

She rested her head against the steering wheel while adrenaline powered through her body, making her pulse pound madly in her ears.

"Was that as dangerous as I thought it was?" she managed finally.

"Worse," he said, laughing with relief. "No one could have handled it better, Jill. No one."

"I really did it, didn't I?" she asked in wonder.

He playfully touched her hand, her forearm, then his own. "We're here, aren't we? That's all thanks to your driving."

"I've never done anything like this in my entire life," she said, turning to him. "There's always been someone else around to bail me out." Her life in Palm Beach had been protected, pampered, positively safe. Even the loss of her baby had been a quiet loss, something that happened within the sterile white walls of a dignified hospital and was over before she could grasp the enormity of the event.

In twenty-six years she'd never been challenged on this level; two weeks ago she wouldn't have believed she could rise to that challenge.

Now she was beginning to think she could do anything.

Her emotions sailed high as the mountains that surrounded them, and she let out a whoop of triumph. Her adrenaline level went up another notch.

"Thank you!" she cried, throwing her arms around Tony's neck. "If you hadn't been here I wouldn't have known what to do."

His voice was low and amused. "You would have managed fine without me," he said as she felt his arms pull her closer to him across the shift. "You can do anything you want, boss lady. It's about time you realized that."

Suddenly she realized that "doing anything you want" had encompassed throwing herself into the arms of her erstwhile employee.

Embarrassed, she put her hands on his chest—taking note of the hardness of the muscle and the warmth of the body—and tried to extricate herself from both the posture and the predicament.

"Adrenaline," she apologized. "What can I say?"

She waited for him to slap her face and tell her to keep her hands to herself, which was exactly what she liked to think she'd have done if the situation were reversed.

And, if he wanted to pay her back for the terrible things she'd said to him earlier in their association, he could scream "Sexual harassment!" and take her to court.

Wouldn't that be wonderful, explaining to some stern father-figure judge that she hadn't really meant to put her hands on her employee, it had just seemed the thing to do at the moment.

Of course, he didn't do either of those.

He just looked at her quietly and long, and it occurred to her that his eyes were the color of the pines that blanketed the sides of the mountains, that deep endless green that changed with the sun and moon, and she wondered why it had taken her so long to appreciate something so obviously extraordinary.

The silence deepened between them. The truck's engine rumbled pleasurably but it seemed terribly far away to Jill, as if it were floating toward her from another universe. Clear, early spring sun streamed through the windows—despite the warning of a possible storm farther north—and brought out red and amber highlights in his dark hair.

The moment grew heavy with promise until she found it difficult to draw a breath. The right-hand corner of his mouth drew upward slightly, and the faint shadow of a dimple flickered in his cheek then disappeared.

It was all up to her.

She had but to lean forward and close that space between them and the kiss they were both imagining would become real in an instant.

But kisses were not meant to be contemplated; they were meant to be shared. The electricity in that truck crackled and snapped and finally faded, and Jill laughed ruefully and drew away from him.

"Why don't you drive?" she asked as her pulse rate went back to normal.

"Anything you say, boss lady."

His smile told her he was a man of his word.

Dangerous, she thought. Very dangerous.

If she'd only had the nerve . . .

AN HOUR LATER they pulled into a truck stop called Lina's Greasy Spoon Café that, unfortunately, lived up to its tongue-in-cheek name. Lina's boasted a counter with four stools, three of which were broken. The fourth was a garish red vinyl cracked across the top and mended with shiny brown packing tape.

Not a good sign.

Lina, a large woman draped in an unlikely pale blue kimono and red-and-white checkered apron, waved them toward the six tables scattered haphazardly around the small café.

One of the tables was occupied by a weary trucker dozing over his grilled cheese sandwiches. Another boasted two cowboys—who looked old enough to pre-date barbed wire—arguing loudly over a game of checkers, punctuating their statements with periodic blasts toward the spittoon at their feet.

An unlikely image of the Emory Club flashed through his brain, and he laughed out loud.

Next to him, Jill was horrified.

"I refuse," she stated flatly. "I absolutely refuse."

"Local color," he said as her face turned the green of wilted lettuce. "Where's your sense of adventure?"

"My sense of adventure ends where ptomaine begins."

He gestured toward Lina who was flipping flapjacks with mad abandon. "She might be a terrific cook. Look at that wrist action."

"Wrist action and salmonella go hand in hand."

"Scrambled eggs," he urged. "What can it hurt?"

"Forget it," she said turning greener.

"We've got a long drive ahead of us," he said. "That bed-and-breakfast place Hank found is at least one hundred and fifty miles away from here."

She hesitated. "I don't know...."

"Trust me," he said. "Have I steered you wrong yet?"

She was still laughing as she disappeared in search of a clean bathroom.

However, she wasn't laughing a half hour later when he spread their impromptu picnic lunch in front of her.

Lina may not have approved of his order but the woman went out of her way to put together a picnic second to none. He'd prudently avoided some questionable choices and ended up with an eclectic selection of fruits and vegetables, bread and cheese that was a hell of a lot better than the steady diet of cheeseburgers and Pepsi that they'd been living on.

"You're a genius!" Jill reached immediately for an apple and a wedge of deep yellow cheddar. "How did you manage to get Brunhilde in there to part with her bounty?"

"Would you believe I flirted with her?"

Jill, mouth filled with fruit, shook her head.

He laughed and grabbed for a hunk of rye bread and some Swiss cheese. "Good," he said, "because I don't think she would have bought that approach. All I did was tell her what I wanted."

"That's it?"

"Well, that and a ten dollar surcharge."

"Capitalism," Jill said ruefully. "Is it great or what?"

Capitalism, however, might have provided the meal but it could never have provided the ambience. He'd found a spot about a mile down from Lina's that was off the road.

Tucked between two bluffs sharper than a ranchhand's profile, this was a small piece of primitive beauty that had somehow survived the onslaught of the twentieth century.

Even though it was early spring, a crisp wind whistled around them but the cold was more than compensated for by the beautiful flowers beginning to dot the horizon. Jill told him about the lupine and wildflowers and snowdrops that swept the land with ruby and gold and cornflower blue, and he found himself wishing he had more than thirty days to live this odd and wonderful life.

His emotional foundation was melting and changing shape same as the pools of winter snow that filled the eddies.

"You're quiet," Jill said, polishing off the rest of the cheddar and reaching for the Pepsi she seemed unable to live without. "Is my nature talk boring you?" It was said without the edge that had marked so many of their early conversations.

He didn't say anything, mainly because he didn't trust his voice. Instead he pointed toward the eastern sky where a hawk soared with the grace of one born to fly. Man was a poor comparison.

Not Jill, however. The more time he spent with her—unavoidable, given their situation—the more he found himself drawn to her.

Last night he'd been feeling wide-awake and restless and so he pushed on, driving well past midnight. The only light on the dark ribbon of road came from his headlights and the blanket of stars overhead, and yet somehow Jill seemed to glow with a light all her own.

She was curled up on the passenger's seat, as comfortable as the seat belt would allow. She slept quietly, her breathing a hushed sibilance in the cab, a soft benediction to his ears. Her breasts rose and fell to the gentle rhythm of her breathing, and he wanted to be the silky sweater that clung to the beauty he had so far only imagined. He wanted to be the pale blond hair drifting across her cheek, caressing her skin.

Damn it. It was impossible to be so close to her, to see her with that shield of independence and strength lowered, and not want to pull her into his arms.

It was impossible to see her sweep onto a makeshift stage in Duck Bluff or Rudder's Pass in a glittering gown of ice-blue silk with her hair piled atop her head and her beautiful gray eyes serious and determined and not want to ply her with champagne and strawberries and whisk her off to the south of France.

Hell.

It was growing more impossible by the day to remember that theirs was a business arrangement. That she had people and possibilities waiting back in Palm Beach that he probably knew nothing about.

Which was probably a good thing since every time he thought about her being in the arms of another man he felt like slamming the truck into gear and kidnapping her, the two of them disappearing together into a life of impromptu picnics and concerts-to-go.

Suddenly it didn't sound like a half-bad life.

Not if she were in it with him.

"Watch the hawk," she said, a funny note of laughter and curiosity in her voice. "You can watch me anytime."

Not really, he thought, looking at her. Only three more towns left on their current list and after that, who knew?

In his other life, that life of privilege and ease, he would have turned her words around until they were a blatant, unmistakable invitation to share some temporary pleasure. He'd discovered along the way that the easiest way to rid himself of an obsession was to indulge himself until that obsession lost its hold on him.

He would have leaned over and pulled her close to him, whispered in her ear, stroked her shoulder and kissed her mouth, and discovered soon enough that she was a woman like any other. No one magical. No one to make him believe "forever after" was anything but a clever ruse perpetuated by hopeless romantics upon a hapless world.

But this wasn't his other life. This was her life, played by her rules, and he refused to take the easy way out—no matter how strong the temptation.

And maybe just this once he didn't want this obsession to end.

She reached over and touched his arm lightly. "Tony?"

Abruptly he stood up and held out his hand to help her to her feet.

"Come on," he said. "We'd better get back on the road."

Before he got any more lost than he already was.

JILL SHIFTED POSITION in her seat and rested her sneakered feet against the dashboard of the truck. They were about thirty miles out of Devil's Heart where they'd be spending the night.

"Best Christmas?" She popped the top on a can of Pepsi.

Tony's answer was immediate. "1969. We went to Hawaii."

"Hawaii?" She scowled. "Who'd want to spend Christmas watching Santa ride the waves?"

He looked at her. "Beats watching Santa get mugged in Rockefeller Center."

"It's hot in Hawaii," she persisted. "I want to see mistletoe and holly at Christmastime, not orchids and plumeria."

"Plumeria?"

"Little red flowers, and don't change the subject. We're talking about Christmas."

"And I still say my best Christmas was in Hawaii."

"Impossible! There's no snow in Hawaii."

He laughed that deep, rumbly laugh of his, and she tingled from head to toe. "And I suppose there's snow in Palm Beach?"

"We're talking *your* best Christmas, Tony, not mine." How had she managed to get so lucky? A man who liked a good argument as much as she did.

"What did you do?" he asked, grinning broadly. "Make snowballs on the beach?"

"We went to Switzerland," she mumbled out the window.

"I can't hear you."

She turned and glared at him, aware she was in danger of bursting into laughter any second. "We went to Switzerland."

"Gstaad?"

He really was amazing. "You've been reading *Travel and Leisure* again?" she asked.

"You don't have the market cornered, boss lady." He downshifted at the foot of a winding hill. "Your turn: best Christmas?"

"1969."

"You can't be any more original than that?"

"If you want originality, I'll say 1822. If you want honesty, it's 1969. It was the last Christmas I believed in Santa Claus."

He chuckled. "Did Santa carry a Hermes toy sack?"

She poked him in the forearm. "Yes, and his sleigh had a Rolls Royce engine."

The chuckle escalated into another full-bodied laugh.

"Is there something funny about Rolls Royces?"

He shook his head. "Family joke," he said. "I'll explain it to you one day."

Jill shrugged and took a sip of Pepsi. "Best year?"

"Easy." Tony grabbed the can from her and took a swig. "1974."

"1974? Nobody liked 1974."

"I *loved* 1974. Watergate. Presidential resignations. Checkers revisited. Watching all of my dad's staunch Republican friends crying into their martinis."

Jill stared at him. "Republican friends? I would have figured your family for Democrats." There went another of her blue-collar stereotypes.

"My family can't even spell the word *Democrat*," he said with a laugh. "If my father could have found a way to have *Republican* added to my birth certificate, he would have."

"But 1974," she protested. "You were just a kid. Why on earth would you care about Watergate?"

"Because I was fifteen years old and I loved anything that made my father miserable."

"What about your mother? Did that make her miserable, too?"

"My mother died before my first birthday. As far as I know, she was a Republican, too." He turned toward her and grinned. "Your turn," he said. "Best year?"

"1981," she said after a moment. "I'd just gotten married and finished at the Mozarteum and I thought I was going to take the world by storm." She shrugged. "So much for my prognostications."

"Do you still wish you were married?" Tony asked, his voice casual.

"Sure." He turned to look at her, and she laughed. "I loved being married. I just wouldn't want to be married to Craig again."

"Why not?"

It was an outrageously personal question but somehow she had given him the right to ask it. "Because I discovered one very important thing: It never works when one partner loves more than the other."

"And you loved him more than he loved you?"

"Afraid so." She drank some more soda. "How about you? Ever been married?"

"Who, me? I'm not marriage material," he said. "Strictly temporary help."

Listen to him, you fool. He's telling you something.

"Hit and run?" There was a subtle edge to her voice that she simply couldn't smooth over. Somehow she knew his flip words hid underlying truths.

"Ugly words, Wiley. I've never gotten involved with a woman who didn't understand exactly what the score was."

"Ugly words, Graham," she snapped back. "You make it sound like a spectator sport."

"Spectator sport?" That grin of his was back in place. "Not if you do it right."

A series of detailed images of the two of them doing it right flashed before her eyes.

"You're blushing," he said.

She fanned herself with some sheet music. "It's hot in here."

"It's seventy-two in here and holding steady. The old man sprang for climate control, remember?"

Damn Hank and his obsession with details anyway.

"So maybe I like it colder," she said.

He laughed. "Best temperature?"

"Sixty-five." She tossed the empty soda can into a paper bag by her feet. "Best first date?"

"Contradiction in terms," he said. "There is no such thing as a best first date. First dates are strictly pass/fail propositions."

She thought about her own few first-date experiences since her divorce. "You have a point there."

He eased the truck into low as they climbed higher. "Best day?"

She looked at him, and something inside her heart melted.

This one, she thought. *Best year, best month, best minute.*

Chapter Eight

Unfortunately, the best of times didn't last forever.

By the time they got to Devil's Heart that evening, she was beginning to feel the heaviness building in her lower abdomen, the sign that her unpredictable period was about to make one of its rare appearances. If she'd been alert, she would have recognized the signs: the bone-deep lassitude that had taken hold that afternoon and the way she'd found herself on the verge of stupid, pointless tears.

Hormones, she thought as Tony guided the truck into a tight parking space behind the B & B where Hank had made reservations for them. Her hormones were running amok inside her body and turning her into a roiling mass of contradictory emotions that she couldn't identify, much less control.

The sky had grown ominously dark, and the weather forecasts talked about a spring snowstorm bearing down on them from the north—a possibility she refused to consider.

Next to her, Tony turned off the engine and yawned. "A steak," he said, "charcoal-broiled, medium-rare. Baked potato. Then oblivion."

"Brandy," said Jill as she climbed out of the truck and took a breath of icy mountain air. "A snifter of brandy and a bubble bath. That's my idea of paradise on earth."

"Good thing you don't play tonight," he said, pulling their suitcases out of the truck. "I don't think I could move a harmonica."

She laughed tiredly. "Don't feel bad. I'd fall asleep with my nose resting on middle C."

She followed him into the small sitting room that served as the lobby.

"You register," he said, depositing the bags next to her. "I'll go check out the dinner menu."

Jill stood patiently for a few moments, admiring the quaint, flowered wallpaper, the chintz-covered loveseats, the brass reading lamp over by the wing chair in the corner. Finally she coughed politely and was rewarded by a cry of "Comin'! Comin'! Just hold your horses!"

A small, round woman with a head of unbelievably perfect, white finger curls bounced into the room, took one look at Jill and scowled. "No rooms," she said tersely. "No rooms for a hundred miles."

Talk about a warm welcome.

"A hundred miles?" Jill asked, her interest piqued.

The woman looked at her as if she couldn't believe Jill's stupidity. "The blizzard's comin'," she said, nodding her head until her curls bobbed up and down in chorus. "It's comin'. If I were you I'd be goin' back where I came from before I got snowbound."

A Floridian born-and-bred, Jill had trouble believing in springtime blizzards. "I appreciate your concern, but all I'd like right now is my room."

"Told you we ain't got any vacancies."

"I'm sorry," Jill said, stifling another yawn. "I didn't make myself clear. We have reservations."

"I don't take reservations."

"I'm afraid you took this one," Jill persisted, her temper rising. "Two single rooms with a bath." The woman said nothing. "The names are Graham and Wiley."

"No reservations," the woman repeated. "And even if I had 'em, you'd be out of luck. Ain't no rooms open no matter how you cut it."

"Would you check your books, please?"

The woman's sigh filled the tiny lobby. "I told you, miss, there ain't no book 'cause I don't take reservations."

A knot of tension added to the cramps in her midsection. "You're sure?"

She must have looked pretty pathetic because the woman lost her combative edge and actually looked human for the first time. "Wish I could oblige you, miss, but it just ain't gonna be." The clerk brightened. "Besides, you wouldn't want to be stranded here in Devil's Heart, a pretty city girl like you."

The thought of being stranded in a quaint inn with Tony Graham had its charm; the thought of being stranded in the truck with PMS swooping down on her along with a crazy spring blizzard had none.

"Where are the pay phones?" she asked. What she needed to do was call Hank. He'd be able to straighten this all out.

If she knew anything about Tony Graham it was the fact he had the world's worst sense of direction. There was a good chance they were at the wrong inn—and it was even money they were even in the wrong town.

She went outside to call the ranch.

THE DINNER MENU WAS SPARTAN but at that point saw-
dust à la mode sounded like manna from heaven to
Tony. He was surprised to see the crowd in the minus-
cule dining room; who would have thought the entire
population of Devil's Heart would have decided to all
go out to dinner the same night?

But then they did things differently in small towns,
didn't they? Maybe this was some kind of rural ritual
that had escaped him.

He hurried back to the lobby to get Jill and found the
room empty, save for their two suitcases which still
rested to the right of the desk where he'd left them.
Maybe she'd left her American Express card in the truck
and had gone out to retrieve it.

She wasn't going to have much success since he had
the only set of car keys so he was heading toward the
parking lot when he saw her at the pay phone near the
rear door.

Her slender body was cupped over the receiver as if
to shield it from the wind whipping around the side of
the building. Sitting with her hour after hour in the
confines of the truck's cab he tended to forget how delicately made she was. The sight of her small but beautifully proportioned body brought with it a rush of
desire that nearly knocked him off his feet.

Tonight, he thought, watching her hair blowing
wildly around her head, his fatigue suddenly forgotten.
Tonight he'd tell her what he was feeling, what he'd
been feeling since the first moment he met her.

Tonight he wouldn't be her employee. He would take
her to dinner and buy her champagne and they would
be a man and a woman together.

For days he'd wanted to touch her, to feel the silki-
ness of her hair beneath his lips, the softness of her skin

against his fingertips, the soft rush of her breath as she murmured his name.

But what terrified him the most, what filled him with hope and fear and sweet desire, was how close they had become—and how quickly it had happened.

In the space of a heartbeat she'd become the center of his life, a life he'd never known was empty until he tried to envision it without her.

He walked up to her just as she was hanging up the phone. His heart hammered against his rib cage like a caged animal. Tonight he'd—

"I have to go back to Palm Beach." Her face was ashen; her eyes, dark as the storm clouds gathering.

He was finding it hard to hear her over the rush of blood pounding in his ears. "You what?"

"I have to go back," she repeated, her voice thin and tight. "Pa's in the hospital."

She started to shake uncontrollably, and he gathered her to him until her head rested against his chest. How often had he fantasized this moment?

With one slight exception.

"What happened?" He still hadn't recovered from the maniacal way the old man drove. An accident wasn't inconceivable.

"Heart attack," Jill said. "Can you believe that? Never been sick a day in his life and—" She shook her head and bit back her words.

"How bad is it?"

"Mother says he's fine, but I have to see him for myself. He's always been there for me, always been the one who understood. If anything happens—"

"Shh," said Tony, brushing a tear off her cheek with his index finger. "Nothing's going to happen to him. That man will live to be a hundred." He had to. Hank

Wiley was ornery and opinionated and hell-on-wheels to work for, but Tony liked him better than ninety-nine percent of the people he'd ever come in contact with.

LUCK WAS WITH THEM.

Somehow Tony managed to keep them just ahead of the storm and ten hours after leaving Devil's Heart, he handed the keys to the truck over to Don Livingston, one of Pa's ranchhands. Jill stood there in front of the American Airlines terminal at McCarran and watched as their home for the past two weeks disappeared into the Vegas morning.

She'd already called the hospital at Palm Beach and learned that Hank's condition had been upgraded to satisfactory and he was out of CCU. And, painful though it was, she'd written out a check that covered Tony's back pay and severance wages that he'd pocketed without even glancing at the numbers—a gesture that endeared him to her even more.

Tony put his arm around her shoulders, and they walked back into the terminal. From the second she told him about the change of plans, Tony had been supportive and sympathetic and—well, "wonderful" said it best.

They'd even managed to avoid their usual "no, no, that's east not west, you idiot" battles when he'd handed her their battered map and let her plot their course back to Las Vegas.

If it hadn't been for Pa, she would have made certain they never got there....

"Flight 87 to West Palm. Now boarding at Gate 2."

Damn the loudspeaker.

How was she ever going to say goodbye to Tony Graham?

She fumbled for words. "You won't forget to cancel the rest of our shows?" she asked for the tenth time as they approached Gate 2. "Everyone's been so nice—I don't want to disappoint them." *I don't want to say goodbye to you.*

"I have two hours until my flight leaves. I'll take care of everything."

"Don't forget the piano tuners. Make sure you call them." She hesitated then whipped a piece of paper and a pen from her bag. "Maybe I should give you my private number, just in case—"

"You worry too much, boss lady," he said, his voice soft. He looked down at the paper she gave him for a moment then put it in his back pocket. "I'm not going to let you down."

"I know." The yearning in her voice horrified her. She might just as well lay her foolish heart at his feet. Instead, she extended her hand, all business. All lies. "Thank you for everything, Tony. I'm sorry this scheme of mine didn't work out. We were just beginning to hit our stride."

His grip was strong and warm. Tears filled her eyes, and she looked down, cursing Eve for giving into temptation and making women so damned vulnerable to moments like this.

"Just set it up again," he said, "and I'm yours."

She could think of nothing to say. Pa, after all, had been the one who put it all together, and now that he was laid up in the hospital, who knew how long it would be before he was well enough to tell her how he did it all so quickly. By that time, she'd just be a job reference to Tony Graham.

No, she recognized the end when she saw it.

And this most definitely was the end.

"Last call!" the loudspeaker blared.

"I'd better go," she said. When on earth was he going to break their handshake? "It's hard enough to get a flight out on a Saturday..."

He started to say something; she heard the quick, low sound in his throat as he caught his words. She glanced toward the gate as the last of the passengers disappeared through the jetway entrance.

"Tony? I—"

Tony Graham, her employee, said, "Shut up, boss lady," then pulled her into his arms and kissed her.

"Come with me!" The words were out before she could wish them back, safely hidden inside her heart. "We should talk. We should—"

My God, but his mouth was sweet, deliciously cool against her fevered lips, his breath intimate and warm against her cheek. The juxtaposition of contrasts made her dizzy with longing.

"This isn't the end," he said, meeting her eyes. "I promise you that."

"I'd give anything to stay here, Tony, but Pa—" She stopped, torn between love of family and the deep, violent surge of desire that seemed to make it impossible for her to be anything but honest.

Dangerously honest.

He pulled her close for one long, heartbreaking moment then let her go, and she watched as he walked away from her, down the long, shining, empty corridor, until he turned a corner and disappeared.

It wasn't until she landed in West Palm that she realized his parting words were, "You haven't seen the last of me."

How much she wanted to believe that....

MANHATTAN
Two days later

"UNBELIEVABLE," Antony Graham Wellington III said for the second time. "Gentlemen, I give you my son, the truck driver."

Tony looked over at his father, and his father's poker playing pals. What was unbelievable was the fact that nothing ever changed. His whole life had been turned inside out, and his father was still playing penny-ante poker with millionaires.

"An affront to his lineage," Wellington the elder continued, obviously enjoying the audience. "If he were cut out for that life, he would have won the bet."

Messrs. Brewer and Brody nodded sagely and upped their bets.

Tony looked over at his father. "Stuff it, Dad," he said evenly, then went back to his stack of northern Nevada phone books.

"Such insolence!" Sloane-Thompson, whose stack of chips had been steadily dwindling all afternoon, grinned at Tony. "I'd send him to the sauna without his trust fund."

The other men laughed.

All of them, that is, except Tony's father.

"You've already lost the bet, Antony. You can stop this man-of-the-people charade." He fanned his cards face-up on the table and raked in his winnings. "And I fully expect you to uphold your part of the bargain."

Tony scribbled the name of the mayor of Devil's Heart in a leather-bound notebook.

"You'll get your damned Rolls," he said. "Now, butt out."

"Butt out?" His father's voice registered his shock. "This is what I invested a fortune in a Yale education for? This is what I . . ."

Tony tuned him out the same way he used to tune him out when he was sixteen years old and his father was lecturing him on the ways of women when what he'd needed was advice on girls.

For the last day and a half, Tony had been attempting to compile a list of contacts who could help him piece together Jill's aborted tour. Living on caffeine and telephone calls, he'd spoken to mayors and music teachers, county clerks and clever businessmen, all of whom promised him everything but had yet to deliver one damned thing.

Since saying goodbye to Jill, he'd been on fire, obsessed with the need to see her again. Sure he knew he could call her on her private line and fill her head with the cheap and pretty talk that had always done well by him, but this time a phone call wouldn't be enough.

Flying to Palm Beach for dinner and dancing wouldn't do it.

None of the mindless, empty rituals he was known for even came close.

This was the real thing, and Tony had no idea how to handle it.

His entire world had been tilted upside down, and he had no idea how to right it—and even less inclination to try.

He wanted to see Jill first thing every morning with her pale blond hair scooped back into a ponytail and her face free of makeup.

He wanted to argue with her over each left turn and laugh at her jokes and stand backstage in each of those damned little one-horse towns and cheer her on as that Juilliard education was finally put to use.

Damn it to hell!

Who was he trying to kid?

What he wanted was exactly what they'd been sharing those ten days on the road.

He wanted her, Jill Wiley, and every damned thing that came with her, including that crazy cowboy of a grandfather of hers.

"Are you in or are you out?" his father asked as he started to deal.

"Out," said Tony, underlining the names of four members of the Silver Canyon Chamber of Commerce. "Forget I'm here."

"Would that I could," mumbled Antony III. "My son has gone mad," he announced to the table in general. "Undeniably mad. A truck driver, indeed...."

Sloane-Thompson picked up his cards, smiled slightly, then looked over at Tony. "What's her name?" he asked.

"Jill," said Tony. He stood up, collected his books and papers and met his father's eyes. "Have fun, gentlemen."

It was the first time in the history of the weekly Emory Club poker game that Antony Graham Wellington III was left speechless.

TONY WAS IN THE BAR of the Emory Club when his father found him an hour later.

"Cut your game short?" he said over his Scotch and tonic. "Or did Max finally win one?"

His father motioned for Robertson, the venerable butler, to bring him his usual then settled back in a worn leather wing chair.

"Max received a call from London. We decided to take a breather."

Tony waited, but his father didn't elaborate.

He'd wanted his father to track him down to the bar; he'd been counting on it. But now that his father had, Tony felt as distanced from him as he always had.

Tell me the secret, he thought, wishing he'd been born to Ozzie Nelson or Bill Cosby, those paragons of American fatherhood.

Antony III lit a cigarette.

You've been in love, Dad. How did it feel? How can I be sure?

Of course, he said none of that. That wasn't their way and, after twenty-eight years of silence, Tony wasn't able to change. Unfortunately, neither was his father.

"So what happened with Rafaela?" Antony III asked after Robertson deposited his tumbler of Drambuie on the rosewood table to his right. "I thought she was your latest inamorata."

"Raf went to L.A. She has a movie offer."

"Are you still seeing her?"

Tony took a long gulp of Scotch. "Curiosity at this late date? Where were you when I was in high school?"

The elder Wellington shook his head and adjusted his right shirt cuff, the way he always did when on the spot. "This is known as conversation, not confrontation. I thought we might give it a try."

I don't want conversation. I want us to really talk.

"So who is she?"

Tony dissembled. "Who is who?"

"Jill. The woman you mentioned to Parker."

"Does it matter?"

"You tell me. You looked fairly serious back there."

It was Tony's turn to say nothing.

"It's about time you thought about settling down, starting your own family," his father continued. "Long overdue. I'd hate to see you miss out on that experience."

Tony's laugh was sharp and sudden. "I know how much you enjoyed the experience."

"That's uncalled-for."

Tony leaned across the table. "Maybe so. Why don't you elaborate on the joys of family life then, Dad? Try to convince me." *I want to understand what it's all about. I want you to help me.*

He waited while his father drained his Drambuie and lit another cigarette. Finally he pushed back his chair and stood up. "That's about what I thought. I'll let you get back to your card game, Dad."

Tony headed for the door and was halfway down the stairs to the foyer when his father's voice reached him.

"Tony?"

He stopped on the landing and looked up. His father stood leaning over the railing, drenched in a flood of pale yellow sunshine from the huge window behind him.

"What?" *Ask me to stay. Let's put all the crap aside and find out what makes us tick.*

But the moment for understanding disappeared the same way it always had in the past.

"Dad? Is there something you want?"

Antony III shook his head and tapped his signet ring against the banister. "Take care, Son." Then he turned and disappeared.

"You, too, Dad," Tony said.

He hit the street and was halfway down Fifth Avenue when he realized his father had called him "Son" for the first time in years.

It was small, but it was something.

PALM BEACH
Four days later

"HELLFIRE, GIRL!" HANK ROARED from his hospital bed. "What's with that long face? I ain't dyin', am I?"

"You?" Jill pushed aside a stack of magazines, two boxes of candy and a basket of fruit large enough to feed the Miami Dolphins, and sat down in the chair opposite him. "How could you die? With that ornery temper of yours, you'll be around until you're one hundred and twenty. I don't know how Mary puts up with you."

"Mary Small is a good woman," Hank said, "and a good woman always stands by her man."

Jill grinned at him but said nothing as a nurse bustled in to take his blood pressure. Mary Small had been one of the more pleasant surprises she'd encountered since returning home. Hank's rumored romance was no rumor at all: Her grandfather was head-over-bootheels in love with a dignified Connecticut widow of indeterminate years who thought nothing of giving the redoubtable Hank Wiley a piece of her mind whenever she thought he deserved it.

And that, apparently, was quite often.

He had brought his new friend, Mary Small, down to Palm Beach to take a look at a plane he was thinking of buying from one of Jill's father's friends when he'd experienced some discomfort that he dismissed as a big lunch and Mary wisely identified as a potential problem.

Before Hank could yell "Hands off me, woman!" she whisked him to the hospital where what could have developed into a major cardiac problem was arrested at a much earlier, less dangerous stage.

For that alone, Jill would have loved her.

Mary Small, however, was a terrific woman: warm, witty, occasionally wisecracking. She'd already served notice that she was taking Hank back up to New England with her as soon as he was discharged from the hospital and going to subject him to some no-nonsense Yankee care.

Jill was beginning to get the idea that if things kept on the way they were, Hank's sixth venture onto the stormy seas of matrimony just might be smooth sailing after all.

At least, she hoped so.

It would be nice to see one member of the Wiley family happily remarried.

"Now, out with it, girl," Hank demanded as soon as the nurse swished out of the room in a cloud of perfume and rubbing alcohol. "What did that low-life scoundrel Graham do to you?"

"Low-life scoundrel?" She tried to force a laugh but failed miserably. "You were the one who thought I should hire him."

"Hire him, sure," Hank said, pushing a huge arrangement of yellow tulips and bright red roses out of his way. "I didn't say you had to fall in love with him."

Jill's face flooded with color, and she turned to look out the window, praying her grandfather wouldn't notice.

No such luck.

"I don't hear nothin', Jilly. What have you got to say about that?"

"You hear nothing because I have absolutely nothing to say." Her voice was clipped, her tone terse. Anyone but Hank Wiley would recognize the fact that it was a closed subject.

"Look at me and tell me you haven't fallen in love with that young fella."

Jill turned and looked at her grandfather. "I'm not in love with that young fella. There! Are you satisfied?" Why should he be? She sounded like the worst kind of lovestruck fool. Her grandfather would see through that statement in an instant.

And, of course, he did. "When did it happen?" Hank asked.

Jill got up and walked over to the window, which overlooked Lake Worth. Boats with brightly colored sails bobbed in the spring breeze. Lovers strolled hand in hand along the water's edge, spinning sweet stories of innocence and optimism.

She quickly turned away.

"Beside a swimming pool behind a motel in Branchwater," she said finally. "Can you imagine that?" Her laugh was soft, bemused.

Hank's laugh was anything but. "'Course I can imagine that," he bellowed. "Branchwater's where I met my third wife...or was it my second? Hell, it don't make no difference. Branchwater's as good a place as any to fall in love."

"I haven't said I fell in love, Pa."

"You ain't said you haven't neither, girl."

She threw her hands in the air. "Okay, okay! So I fell in love. What of it? It's over and done with, and I don't even have any wonderful romantic memories to take with me in my old age. He's gone his way and I've gone mine and that's that."

She sat back down in the chair and dared him to pursue the topic any further.

He did. "You just gonna let it go at that, girl?"

"What else can I do? Fly up to New York and camp on his doorstep with my heart in my hand?"

"Hire him back," Hank said.

"To do what? Clean our swimming pool? He's a bright man, Pa. He'd see right through that."

"Hire him back to continue your tour. Hell, girl, you ain't even half done."

"But we cancelled all of our dates." She could hear her words to Tony as clearly as if they were on tape. "I made a point of asking him to take care of that."

"So uncancel them!" Hank roared. "Girl, you're a sorry imitation of a Wiley if you can't see the writin' on the wall. You gotta go for what you want in life. It ain't never gonna just show up on your doorstep."

"But you don't even have your list of contacts with you, Pa," she protested. That was why her mother hadn't been able to leave a message for Jill at one of her stops. "How can we reconstruct it?"

"Tell me where you've been," he said, "and I'll tell you where you're goin'. Ain't nothin' hard about that, is there?"

Taking complete charge of your life was more difficult than she thought. Being a dutiful daughter and an obedient wife hadn't prepared her for anything like this.

What Hank was advocating was as straight-shooting as a Colt .45 and just about as dangerous.

"I can't leave you," she said, grasping at straws. "It wouldn't be right."

"Stayin' behind for an old man who has his own woman is what wouldn't be right. We each gotta do what we gotta do, Jilly. And if it takes more than one shot to find the right one, then that's the way it is."

She looked at her grandfather, a man who had courted dangers of the heart since the day he was born and still loved life more than anyone she'd ever known. If Tony Graham didn't turn out to be the man she thought he was, then she'd chalk it up to experience.

Not giving them the chance to find out would be the greatest tragedy of all.

"Okay, Pa, I have an hour before my appointment," she said grabbing a pad and pen from his nightstand. "Let's start with Devil's Heart."

He smiled wider than the country that gave birth to him. "That's my girl! You ain't got nothin' to lose by tryin'."

He was one hundred percent right.

The only thing she could lose was her heart, and she had the feeling that had already been lost somewhere west of Branchwater.

DR. BEAUMAN, a ruddy-faced man with a perfectly trimmed white mustache, was jotting notes on her chart when Jill came back into his office.

"Sit down," he said, smiling up at her. "I'll be right with you."

Jill nodded and rearranged the skirt of her linen dress as she took the seat opposite him. How little things changed. This had always been the worst part: the waiting.

She could stand the examination table and the stirrups and the pinch of cold metal on vulnerable flesh without flinching, but the second she sat down by Beauman's desk, her legs began to tremble and a burning rock of fear settled deep inside her belly.

"You look like you're about to bolt and run, Jillian," he said, at last. "Relax."

"Easy for you to say." She took a deep breath and clasped her hands loosely on her lap. "So, what's the latest?"

He removed his wire-rimmed glasses and rubbed the two red spots on the bridge of his nose. "I wish I could offer you something positive, Jillian, but there's been no change."

Don't cry, you fool. This is exactly what you expected. "I thought perhaps because my period came, it might mean—"

"I know what you thought, Jillian, and I'm sorry."

She waved her hand in the air as if none of this mattered a damn. "I didn't really believe anything had changed," she said, trying to convince herself, if not her doctor. "I just wondered...." Her voice trailed off.

The doctor went on to detail the state of her health. Her odds of pregnancy were still a thousand to one. "You're hale and hearty," he said, capping his pen and leaning back in his chair. "Except for this one thing, you're a perfect specimen. If I were you, I'd be out having the time of my life. You've spent way too long worrying, Jillian. Things have a way of working out; they did for your mother, and they will for you, too." He cited three other cases of successful adoption, and she finally had to laugh.

"Let me think about finding a husband first, Dr. B.," she said, collecting her purse and rising from her chair.

"It's a new world, Jillian. We're not bound by the old morality, the old ways of thinking." He walked her to the door. "Just keep your options open. Your life is just beginning."

His words stayed with her all the way home.

Your life is just beginning.

Hadn't she been feeling that way since the day she met Tony Graham?

AGNETA POUNCED ON JILL the moment she came through the front door.

"What did Dr. Beauman have to say?"

"Hello, Mother," she said, leaving her purse on the hall table. "Wonderful to see you, too."

Agneta waved away her daughter's sarcasm. "I know you went to see Dr. Beauman," she said, following Jill up the curving staircase toward her bedroom. "Your Uncle Bradley saw you going into his office. Are you all right?" She floated right into the room behind her daughter, a silk-and-satin radar trap. "You haven't looked well since you returned."

Jill kicked off her shoes and sat down on her bed. "There's nothing new, Mother. He just told me to come in for an exam after my next period, and since it decided to make an unexpected appearance this week, I thought I'd follow his advice for a change."

"And?" Agneta's eyes were wide with apprehension.

"And what?" Jill countered. "I'm healthy, regularly irregular and no, nothing's changed."

Except for these painful trips to Dr. Beauman, she'd managed to give up thinking about it, dreaming of it, wishing for it. If she'd learned anything from Hank Wiley, it was the value of reality.

"As long as you're healthy," her mother said, patting her hand. "That's all I care about." A pause, then: "Are you going out with Tyler tonight?"

Jill groaned and flopped back on the bed. "Are you working as his agent now, Mother? I swear, John Alden never had a better middleman."

"He's called three times today," Agneta went on, obviously choosing to ignore Jill's sarcasm once again. "He has tickets for the symphony."

Jill made a face.

"You love the symphony." Her mother stared at her as if she were an alien. "You've always loved the symphony."

"The last thing I feel like doing is putting on the beaded dress and the makeup and the heels and being cooped up with a roomful of people who are more interested in gossip than good music."

"Jill!" Her mother acted as if she'd committed high treason. "What on earth happened while you were in Nevada? You're sounding more like your grandfather every day."

"I'm spoiled now, Mother. Now I know what it's like to play for an audience who really wants to hear you. There's no substitute for that."

She thought she'd been subtle but apparently there was no such thing as being subtle around her mother, for Agneta caught on instantly.

"You're not planning on going back out there, are you?"

"Afraid so."

"I should go over there and give your grandfather a piece of my mind. Of all the ridiculous, absurd..."

Jill's private phone rang, and Agneta instantly brightened.

"Tyler!" she said, grabbing her daughter's arm. "I knew he'd call again. Now when he asks about the symphony, please—"

It rang a second time.

"Mother!" Jill protested. "Let me answer it."

"Don't be rash, darling," Agneta cautioned. "Let it ring once more, then please reconsider about the symphony. You can never—"

Jill broke free from the maternal death grip and motioned for her mother to leave her in peace. Agneta stood in the doorway, a study in breathless anticipation. "Really, Mother, I'm beginning to wonder if you aren't carrying a torch for Tyler yourself. I'm not picking this up until you leave. My answering machine can handle it instead."

She didn't look forward to saying no to Tyler Austin, especially in front of an audience of one extremely biased mother.

But Tyler was a good man and he deserved better than lukewarm affection. She braced herself while her mother closed the door, then picked up the phone. "Hello?"

"How're you doin', boss lady?"

A voluptuous shiver rose up from the center of her body, and she instinctively brought the phone closer.

"Hi," she said, her voice sounding unabashedly soft and receptive. "How are you?"

"The question is, how's your grandfather?"

"Pa's doing wonderfully." She told him about Mary Small and Hank's incredible good fortune. "Leave it to Pa to turn a heart attack into a full-fledged romance."

Tony's deep rumbling laugh brought on another wave of shivers. She was in much deeper than she thought.

"So, what's up?" she asked. "Was there a problem with the check I gave you?"

"Hell, no."

"Did you remember to cancel the piano tuners?"

"Hell, yes."

"Then what's the problem?"

"Remember Devil's Heart?"

"Of course, I do. It was only a few days ago, Tony."

"What would you say if I told you you're booked there again the end of this week?"

She sat straight up. "What?"

"You heard me. I arranged three new bookings. Devil's Heart is the first. Have one of Hank's ranchhands bring the truck to the airport, and we can leave directly from Vegas tomorrow."

"You have a lot of nerve, Graham." A huge smile spread across her face, and she struggled to gain her composure. "What gave you the right to do something like that?" *I wanted to be the one to surprise you.*

"No one," he said, his usual arrogant—wonderful—self. "Take it or leave it, Wiley. They want you and your Mozart-to-go, and I'm willing to go along for the ride. The choice is yours."

Of course, there was no choice at all.

From the second she heard his voice, her decision had been a foregone conclusion.

"Same salary as before?" she asked.

"Same salary."

"Same terms?"

"Different," he said.

"Such as?"

"I'll drive you," he said, same as he'd said a few weeks ago. "I'll move that piano for you. When we're on the road, you're the boss, no questions asked."

"And when we're not on the road?"

"When we're not on the road, boss lady, we play by different rules: mine."

She thought of that kiss in the airport and closed her eyes against an onslaught of vivid fantasies. "Winner take all?" she whispered.

"Winner take everything." Again that deeply sensual laugh. "So, tell me, boss lady, are you game?"

Foolish question.

She was packed before she hung up the phone.

Chapter Nine

LAS VEGAS

The truck was waiting for Tony when he landed at McCarran.

Don Livingston, one of Hank's men, met him by the luggage carousel and gave him the keys.

"You and Jilly goin' out on the road again?" he asked.

That fact should be pretty obvious but Tony had learned that Hank and his pals liked to state the obvious.

"You got it," he said, thanking Don for bringing the truck in for him. "Devil's Heart, Silver Canyon and Free Republic."

Don nodded, gnawing on a blue toothpick, his dentures clicking with each bite. "Good towns. Knew me a woman in Silver Canyon." He grinned around the toothpick. "Rosie," he said. "Must be dead by now."

With that he turned and strode out of the airport, leaving Tony staring after him in amazement.

What was that he'd said about Hank Wiley being the last of his breed? Apparently there were still a few of his endangered species left.

He checked things out on the truck—not that he understood exactly what he was doing. Then he went back inside the terminal and grabbed a cup of lousy coffee and a soggy English muffin at one of those forgettable airport cafeterias that were as bland as his life before Jill.

He was cool and calm. Totally in control.

After all, it had only been seven days since he'd seen her.

Seven days. One hundred sixty-eight hours.

Well, one hundred twelve hours, if you took away the fifty-six he spent dreaming about her.

No way his life could have been turned inside out in one hundred twelve hours. He'd spent a hell of a lot longer than that at Yale, and Yale hadn't changed him one damned bit.

He went in a cocky, fresh-mouthed preppy brat and came out the same way four years later.

But the facts still remained.

Saying goodbye to her that morning one week ago had awakened latent primal instincts he didn't even know he had. He'd said goodbye to many women in his day. Ending a relationship wasn't anything new to him. It had always meant nothing more than the beginning of a new one.

Yet when she extended her hand in goodbye, he knew that he would see her again even if it meant he had to drive that damned truck through Nevada, Wyoming and Montana in order to do it.

And so there he stood at Gate 12, waiting.

Cool.

Calm.

A different game, he'd said on the phone. Different rules.

His rules.

A man in control.

Until the second Jill Wiley exited the jetway and his palms began to sweat, his heart began to thunder—and he began to realize that the game might be different but this was one set of rules that never changed.

When it came to falling in love, no man was ever in control.

Maybe this wasn't such a good idea after all.

JILL SAW HIM the moment she cleared the jetway.

He was leaning against a railing near the ticket counter, jingling a ring of keys in his left hand and dragging his right hand through his thick, dark hair. Dressed in perfectly pressed khaki pants and his ubiquitous polo shirt, he wasn't anyone's idea of the average truck driver, but if there was anything Jill had learned during their time together, it was that Tony Graham wasn't your average truck driver.

He looked up and caught her eye. The smile he gave her caused her breath to catch in her throat, and she stood where she was and watched, mesmerized, as he walked toward her. He was an offbeat blend of brains and brawn, of lean muscle and male power and—well, there wasn't one average thing about him.

He stopped two feet in front of her. "Good flight?"

"A little turbulence," she said. "Nothing major."

Her body fairly tingled with excitement. The last time they'd been together at this very airport, he'd pulled her into his arms and kissed her, and she'd carried the sweet taste of his mouth with her clear across the country.

His beautiful green eyes met hers. How had she never realized just how long, how curly, his lashes were?

She smiled.

His lips parted slightly.

It was going to happen again, she thought. Now she'd know she hadn't imagined it, that what she was feeling wasn't just the product of too many lonely nights.

She leaned toward him.

He reached down and picked up her carry-on luggage. "How many more?"

"Th-three." Was she going mad?

"Pack light, don't you, boss lady?" Without another word, he turned and started off down the concourse toward the baggage-claim area.

Just because this was exactly what she'd let happen the last time didn't mean she'd be that foolish twice. Trotting along after him like a lovable lapdog was the last thing she intended to do.

She wasn't so out of circulation that she didn't recognize a sexually charged moment when she saw one, and that had definitely been a sexually charged moment. That look in his eyes could have generated enough electricity to put Hoover Dam permanently out of business.

Their phone conversation came back to her.

He'd called her "boss lady." He was carrying her bags. She glanced at her watch. These were definitely normal working hours in any one of the forty-eight contiguous states.

She didn't know what had happened to change his attitude, but if he wanted to play it by the book, then so would she.

It might be a different game, Mr. Graham, she thought, *but it's still one I intend to win.*

She stopped dead in front of the ladies' room. "Graham!" Her voice could have carried from there right back to Palm Beach.

He came to an abrupt halt and turned around. "What's the matter? We're going to get your bags."

She held her ground, arms crossed over her chest, right foot tapping impatiently.

Finally he walked back to where she waited.

"Did I miss something?" he asked. "We're getting your bags then hitting the road. Right?"

"I've just flown five hours across the country."

He looked at her blankly. "So?"

She tilted her head toward the ladies' room. "So, did it ever occur to you I might want to use the facilities?"

"They didn't have a bathroom on the plane? If I remember right, 747s have about six of them."

"And three hundred people queued up to use them." She tucked her purse under her arm. "I'll meet you at the baggage area when I'm finished."

That cocky grin was back. "Anything you say, boss lady."

"And, Tony?"

He turned back toward her again. "Yes?"

"You can stick that 'boss lady' in your ear."

He was still laughing even after the door swung closed behind her.

And, damn it, so was she.

BY THE TIME THEY WERE four hours out of Devil's Heart, Jill was four seconds away from letting out a shriek loud enough to start a rock slide.

The atmosphere in the truck was heavy with tension that grew more emotionally charged with every minute.

Gone was the lighthearted banter.

Gone were the arguments over directions, the spats over rest rooms, the idiotic brawls over "the gas gauge is on E will you please stop now'' that had made their last trip together so much fun.

Face it, Von Eron, Jill thought. Gone was the fun.

She'd flown to Las Vegas in a state of such high excitement she'd barely needed the plane. Oh, the story was she was going back to play for people in Devil's Heart and Silver Canyon, but both she and Tony had known the truth.

They had both returned to Devil's Heart for one reason and one reason only.

Now she was beginning to think that one reason had more to do with her piano than it did anything else.

She slouched down lower in the passenger seat of the truck and forced her eyes shut as Tony maneuvered the truck around one of those hairpin curves she remembered from their trip up to Devil's Heart.

She had to hand it to him: When he said he was going to be all-business during business hours, he wasn't kidding.

Their conversation had been straight from the typewriter of the redoubtable Miss Manners.

When he wanted the map, it was: "Would you check the map for me, please, Jill?"

While they ate breakfast, it was: "The bacon is great, isn't it?"

When she wanted to talk the way they'd talked before, he smiled and turned on the radio.

He was being scrupulously polite, pointedly friendly, maddeningly distant.

She felt as awkward with him today as she had the first morning they set out from Hank's ranch. Could she really have been that wrong about things?

Hard to believe it had been only a week since he'd pulled her into his arms at the airport and given her a kiss that did more for her heart rate than three hours of aerobics.

Hard to believe they were the same people.

"Son of a bitch."

She opened her eyes, expecting to find the truck dangling over the edge of a precipice. "What's the matter?"

"We're almost out of gas."

She sat up straight. "You're joking."

He pointed toward the gas gauge. "Read it and weep, boss lady. The big, red *E*."

"I told you to pull in for gas back in Pine Crossing. You should have listened to me."

He glared at her as he shifted into neutral so he could coast down the hill they were on. "If I listened to everything you say, I'd have left you two hundred miles back."

Jill quickly reviewed her conversational gambits. "You don't like to talk about politics?"

"I hate politics."

"Art? Music? Movies?"

"That was a monologue you were giving me," he said. "I didn't want to interrupt."

She slapped her hand against the dashboard. "Damn you, Graham! It was supposed to be a dialogue but you were too busy playing the strong, silent type that went out of style forty years ago when Gary Cooper was doing it."

"Will you shut up?" he snapped. "I'm concentrating."

She hooted with laughter. "Concentrating? You have to concentrate to roll down a hill?"

"Enjoy yourself," he growled. "We'll see how funny it is when you're pushing this thing to the next gas station."

"When *I'm* pushing this thing? You're the truck driver, not me. If anyone's going to push this thing, it's going to be you."

"If you don't shut up," he said, his voice low and deadly, "by God, I'll leave you here on the side of the road and you can see how good you are at hitchhiking."

They hadn't seen another car for at least two hundred miles.

They *had* seen hawks and eagles and maybe a vulture or two circling overhead.

If the furious scowl on Tony's face were any indication, he just might dump her there, piano and all, and head back to the bright lights of Vegas.

Jill wouldn't put it past him.

Maybe shutting up wasn't the same thing as giving in, she rationalized. Maybe it was more like a brand-new life-saving technique the Red Cross hadn't discovered yet.

She shut up.

Miraculously, she managed to keep her mouth closed as the truck sputtered and coughed when Tony shifted gears as they started up a hill with more twists than an Agatha Christie mystery.

Sweat broke out on his forehead. Three drops trickled down his right temple, and she remembered when he'd obligingly kept her own brow clear when she'd been the one in whose hands their lives rested.

She pulled a Kleenex out of the glove compartment. Turnabout was fair play, wasn't it? She owed him this much at least.

"I'm unarmed," she said, waving the pink tissue in the neutral zone between them. He didn't so much as crack a smile. "Let me—" She moved to wipe the sweat from his temples but he blocked her with a move Chuck Norris would have envied.

"Don't."

"Don't? You're sweating. I just—"

"I'm not sweating."

"Oh, no? I suppose that's just a ladylike glow?"

His look was murderous. "I'm not sweating," he repeated.

She looked up at the roof of the truck. "Don't tell me. Let me guess: It's the sprinkler system."

"Don't push it, Jill."

"Look, I don't want to go flying over that precipice because your macho vanity says unobstructed vision violates some rule of male superiority. The fact is, you're sweating, Graham. Wipe your face."

His head swiveled toward her like Linda Blair's in *The Exorcist*, and the truck veered toward the right. "Watch the road!" she yelled.

"To hell with the road." He stopped right there, halfway up the mountain.

"Why did you stop?"

She glanced out the window and down to the canyon below. "You're making me nervous, Tony."

He leaned back in his seat. "Okay," he said. "Do it."

She stared at him. "Do what?" She'd forgotten testosterone did more than give them those interesting hair patterns and the inability to admit defeat. It also made them crazy. She moved closer to the passenger door. "If you make one move closer, so help me, I'll—"

He laughed out loud. "You flatter yourself, Wiley. You wanted to wipe my face," he said calmly. "So do it."

"You're not sweating anymore."

"I wasn't sweating in the first place."

"This is getting ridiculous," said Jill, crumpling up the Kleenex and stuffing it back in the glove compartment where it belonged. "It's getting dark and we're in the middle of nowhere. Let's get going."

"No," he said.

"Please start the car, Tony."

"Sorry."

"Tony, if you don't—"

He flipped the key to accessory and pointed toward the gas gauge once more. "Read it and weep, boss lady."

Visions of herself pushing a three-ton truck up the incline while Tony Graham napped behind the wheel taunted her. "What now?" she asked in desperation. "Pine Crossing must be a hundred miles back."

He opened his door.

"What are you doing? You can't be serious! Not even a marathoner could handle a hundred miles of mountain road."

He walked around to her side of the truck and flung open her door. "Come on," he said, grabbing her hand. "Out."

She forced a laugh. "Joke's over, Tony. Get back in and start the truck."

"I'm counting to three. One..."

"This is ridiculous! You're acting like a—"

"Two..."

"—total idiot. It's getting late. Let's—"

"Three."

Before she could draw breath, he slid one arm under her derriere and the other under her left arm and hoisted her out of the cab with an impressive display of strength. Before she could comment on it, he unceremoniously dumped her near the edge of the road.

"What's going on?" She straightened the hem of her sweater and tugged at the waistband of her jeans. "Is there a time bomb in there?"

The look he shot her would have stopped anyone but Hank Wiley's granddaughter. "Not anymore."

"Oh, no, you don't! You can't blame this one on me. I'm not the one who ran out of gas."

He didn't even try to defend himself, and Jill had to bite the inside of her cheek to keep from letting out a whoop. So much for that male superiority he put so much stock in.

"You look pretty damned happy for someone stranded on a mountain road."

"This isn't the end of the world. We'll work something out." She pulled a local map out of her back pocket and checked it. "We're in luck. All you have to do is walk two and a half miles up and around that bend to Fire Creek. I'm sure they'll have a gas station." She really wasn't sure about anything, but this didn't seem the time to tell him so.

"There's one problem."

She looked at the map again. "Well, maybe it's three miles. But you—"

"Bingo!" He stepped closer to her. "Not me," he said. "Us."

"Us?"

"Yes. You know, Wiley: you and me. We. Us."

She backed toward the truck. "Someone has to stay here and watch over things."

"From what? A stray coyote? You're coming with me."

"The hell I am. I'm staying here."

He kicked the passenger door closed and glared at her. "You're coming with me."

"Okay, so you don't understand English. *Nyet. Nein. Non.* I'm not coming with you."

He grabbed her hand and started up the hill. "You're coming with me."

"If my husband had treated me this way, I would have divorced him—"

He looked back over his shoulder at her. "You're memory's slipping: You *did* divorce him."

"You interrupted me. I would have divorced him *sooner*." She came to an abrupt stop. "I'm waiting in the truck."

"Listen." Still gripping her wrist, he came closer. "The nearest town might be ten miles from here—it might be one hundred miles."

"It's two and a—"

"God, woman, don't you ever shut up?"

She choked down the words "You're fired." If they were closer to civilization, Tony Graham, no matter how gorgeous he was, would be history.

"Okay," she said. "I'll shut up. But I'm still waiting for your words of wisdom."

He dropped her wrist as if it were on fire. "Okay," he said, backing away. "You win. You're right. I'm wrong. If you want to sit here all day and play snake bait, it's up to you. I'm out of here."

True to his word, he wheeled around and jogged up the hill, around the bend and out of sight.

"To hell with you," she said, returning to the truck. Let him try that reverse-psychology routine on Taffy, the gas-station nymphet. She, for one, wasn't buying it.

Not anymore.

Why should she go off hunting for high-octane when he was the one who ran out in the first place?

Besides, she was the one paying all the bills around here. Maybe it came of owning his own business, but Tony didn't seem to know the first thing about being an employee. Employees were supposed to take orders, not give them.

A sudden wind blew up, and she shivered. The thing to do was climb into the truck where it was warm and safe and—

She lifted the door handle.

Nothing.

She tugged at it.

No dice.

She dashed around to the driver's side.

Of course not.

The perfect Mr. Graham with his devotion to duty would never leave the door unlocked. A stray jackrabbit might wander in.

And, of course, the brilliant Ms. Wiley with her constant attention to detail had been too stupid to have her own set of keys.

Amazing how fast a woman can run when she had a message to deliver.

Tony was barely a half mile away when she caught up with him.

"Changed your mind, boss lady?" He didn't so much as break stride.

"You're fired!" She was panting so hard she sounded like she was in a Lamaze class.

He grinned down at her as they walked. "Too late. I quit about five minutes ago."

"I didn't hear you."

"How could you? You were relaxing back at the truck."

"Great," she said. "Now I don't have to give you severance pay."

He started to laugh. "I was lying," he said. "I didn't quit. You fired me."

Damn him. She wanted to keep her anger at a fever-pitch and there he was throwing straight lines at her when she was too out of breath to take advantage of them.

They walked on in silence, and she couldn't help wondering why arguing with Tony Graham made her feel better than loving her ex-husband ever had.

BY THE TIME THEY PASSED the Fire Creek—2 mi sign, the wind was howling in earnest, and some gunmetal-gray clouds were settling themselves over the mountaintops.

Next to him Jill shivered, and he slipped out of his leather jacket and handed it to her. "Here."

"No," she said, shaking her head. "Thank you."

"Put it on."

"I'd rather not."

He draped it over her shoulders himself and kept walking. He'd never met a woman as quick-tempered and stubborn as Jill Wiley. He supposed it must be the old man's blood passing through her veins that did it. She was different from any other woman he'd ever known, all those beautiful, intelligent women who managed to keep their emotions on an even keel the same way he always had.

At least, the same way he always had until Jill Wiley came into his life.

She pulled his jacket more closely around her, and a few random, erotic thoughts surfaced, surprising him. The past few hours had been so out of synch that he'd forgotten what this trip was all about.

He'd flown to Las Vegas in a fever; he'd actually ached for the feel of her in his arms, the taste of her mouth, the smell of her perfume.

What he should have done—what he'd been planning to do—was pull her into his arms right there at McCarran Airport and make real all that had been promised on the telephone.

But something happened when he first saw her exiting the jetway, something he'd never experienced before.

Something he wasn't certain he ever wanted to experience again.

Lighthearted desire, something with which he was very familiar, took a sharp turn and angled down into feelings he found as difficult to read as their battered Rand McNally road maps.

He'd wanted hearts and flowers; what he got was a barrage of one-liners that ended with "You're fired."

He knew the courtship dance intimately: wine and soft music and even softer words. But this wasn't courtship; this was the battle of the sexes played by two equally matched opponents who both played to win.

And damned if he wasn't having the time of his life.

ARCHIE'S WAS AT THE OUTSKIRTS of Fire Creek, a tiny, one-pump gas station and convenience store that sold high test and cigarettes and *TV Guide*.

By the time she and Tony made their way up the dirt driveway, another spring snowstorm was drifting across the highway. They hadn't said a word to each other for over an hour. The temperature had been dropping rapidly, and she had tried to give him back his jacket but he'd refused and just turned up the collar of his pale blue polo shirt and kept walking toward town.

How he could be so kind—and so infuriating—puzzled Jill, and she'd spent much of their silent walk trying to piece him together with no luck at all.

He finally broke the silence as they approached Archie's. "It looks deserted," he said, gesturing toward the antiquated gas pump out front. "We'd better keep walking."

"Wait!" She brushed snow off the side window of the small building. "There's a light on inside."

"No cars anyplace," he said. "We'd better—"

He stopped, and she turned around to see what was going on. A small, white-haired woman in a cherry-red sweater stood smiling at them from the corner of the building. Two calico cats, kittens really, twined themselves around her Adidas, and a dalmation puppy nestled in her arms.

"Didn't hear your car, folks," she said as she approached. She looked around at the snow-covered gas pump and driveway. "Don't see your car neither."

Tony explained their immediate problem while the kittens delicately sniffed Jill's right ankle.

"Come in, come in," Grace Benson said after they introduced themselves. "I have some water about to boil. Have some hot chocolate, and we'll see about things."

Tony mumbled something about time under his breath, and Jill kicked his ankle when Grace wasn't looking. "Thank you, Grace," she said, following the woman, the puppy and the kittens into the gas station's front office. "I'm so cold I haven't felt my feet for the last hour."

Grace ripped open two packets of Swiss Miss and dumped the contents into a pair of huge earthenware mugs. "Where are you folks bound for again?"

"Devil's Heart," said Tony, scratching the dalmation behind her ear. "And we're behind schedule."

Jill shot him a quelling look that he neatly deflected with a bland smile.

Grace motioned for Jill to take the battered easy chair near the window and steered Tony to the desk chair. "'Fraid you aren't going anywhere tonight. That's a blizzard brewing out there, sure thing."

Tony groaned and leaned back in the swivel chair. "Doesn't this state recognize spring as a valid season?"

"Talk to me about spring come May or June," Grace said, laughing as one of the calicos leaped onto Jill's lap and settled in. "Like I said, you two won't be going anywhere tonight."

"But the truck," Jill said. "We can't just leave it back there."

"We won't," said Grace. "We'll pile into my Jeep after you warm up and we'll take some fuel back, then you can follow me back to town."

The water boiled. Grace filled the mugs, and sweet, chocolate perfume wafted through the room.

"Is there a hotel in Fire Creek?" Jill asked. "Maybe we should call ahead."

Grace laughed heartily. Even the cats seemed amused. "You've never been to Fire Creek, have you? We have many things—a bank and a pharmacy and a food store—but the one thing we don't have is a hotel."

"A motel?" Jill asked, beginning to panic. "We don't need anything fancy." Just two separate rooms because it had become painfully obvious her romantic fantasies had little bearing on reality.

"A driveway would be enough," Tony said. "We can always sleep in the truck."

"No, you can't," Grace announced, handing them each their hot chocolate. "I wouldn't hear of it."

"Oh, Grace," Jill said, catching Tony's eye, "that's a lovely offer, but we just couldn't."

The old woman scooped up the puppy and cuddled her close to her heart. "Sure you could. I have me a big old empty house, and you'd be doing me a favor spending a stormy night there with me."

It reminded Jill of all the wonderful beginnings of a thousand old gothic novels she'd devoured years ago. The huge old house, the wicked storm outside, the slightly dotty woman, the mysterious man and the fearful young virgin—well, it had *almost* all of the elements. She was in favor of the idea, but Tony apparently wasn't ready to commit himself to spending the night in Fire Creek.

Grace closed down the gas station and they—including the menagerie—piled into her dented green Jeep and retraced their way back to the truck. Jill and Grace chatted about the pets and the weather, and Tony maintained a heavy silence in the back seat as the snow continued to fall.

By the time they got the truck started, the snow cover was so thick, and the visibility so limited that even Tony had to admit defeat as they eased back onto the highway behind Grace and her Jeep.

"I guess we're stuck," he said, downshifting as he cast Jill a quick look. "I hope her house has indoor plumbing."

Leave it to a man to think of the mundane in the middle of a gothic romance come-to-life. She sighed and leaned back in her seat, cuddling the calico who had refused to be parted from her close to her heart. "Yes," she said finally, "I guess we're stuck at that."

They followed Grace Benson back to Fire Creek in a silence deeper than the snow outside.

Chapter Ten

From the outside, Grace Benson's house was a triumph of willpower over architecture.

Set on a hilltop on the far side of Fire Creek, the three-story Victorian wonder leaned slightly to the east and sagged slightly to the west and generally looked in need of some tender, loving care. It wasn't hard to see why she wrote moody gothic romances for a living.

This was the kind of house women usually went crazy over, and Jill Wiley was no exception. The curlicues around the door, the window boxes now covered in snow, the gingerbread trim lining the edge of the roof— she loved it all.

Grace showed them into the parlor at the front of the house, and with a cry of delight, Jill gravitated immediately to an old Steinway piano by the bay window.

"You folks make yourselves comfortable," Grace said, as they were greeted by a Siamese cat, an old Labrador retriever and a squawking parrot in a cage by the staircase. "I'll feed the zoo and then we can talk about dinner."

Tony couldn't help it; his eyes strayed to the lopsided curtain rod, the frayed and faded upholstery, the walls that badly needed paint. He came from a world where these things magically repaired themselves, a world where money and time and good workmanship were never a problem.

A world that had very little reality at the moment.

The old woman's eyes were sharp, and she surprised him. "Archie was always the one who made sure the faucets didn't leak and the windows didn't rattle. I was always so busy with my writing that I never learned how to do these things for myself."

"Archie?" asked Tony. "Your husband?"

Grace nodded. "Forty-seven years. I still wake up in the morning and expect to see him bustling around the kitchen making coffee and toast. We had a routine," she said, smiling as Jill ran through a quick series of finger exercises at the piano. "Archie made breakfast. I made lunch. We both made dinner. Worked pretty well, too." She sighed, and Tony saw the glitter of tears in her light blue eyes. "Pay me no mind, Mr. Graham. It's just I still miss him, that old lug. That's why I keep the filling station open; gives me something to do between books and helps me hang on to him a little longer."

Jill approached, and Grace shook off her melancholy. "Listen to me," she said. "An old woman rambling on about her past. You two sit down and rest and I'll whip up something in the kitchen."

"We've been sitting for hours," Jill said to Tony's surprise. "Why don't you let us give you a hand?"

"Yeah," he said, wondering what in hell he would do in the kitchen. "Be glad to help out."

Before he knew what hit him, he was put to work chopping lettuce and tomatoes for a salad while Grace went out back to check on one of her dogs.

He picked up a huge cleaver from the countertop and started to hack away at an innocent head of iceberg.

Jill, hands covered with meatloaf, took one look at him and started to laugh.

"What's so funny?" he demanded, brandishing the knife. "You've never seen a Samurai Saladmaker before?"

"You tear the lettuce leaves," she said, still chuckling. "Not dismember them."

"I find it hard to believe you spent a lot of time in your Palm Beach kitchen."

"You're right," she said, forming the amorphous lump of chopped meat into something resembling a loaf of bread. "But do you think anyone ever had a free ride at Pa's ranch?"

He grinned and started to tear the lettuce leaves into bite-sized pieces. "You have a point, boss lady."

She was Hank Wiley's granddaughter, after all, and obviously used to impromptu meals like this.

Tony most definitely was not. There was a feeling of unity in this kitchen, a sense of time and place that kept him silent during most of the supper. Grace gave them huge bowls of corn chowder with chunks of fresh bread and warm cider that banished memories of Lutece and The Russian Tea Room forever.

Jill and Grace had an easy rapport that Tony envied. Where Tony found it difficult to go beyond banter and small talk with people, Jill Wiley marched right into the heart of things. She talked a little about her marriage, that it was childless and not by choice, and he listened as Grace told them about Archie and how despite their own childlessness, their forty-seven years together had been deep and fulfilling and happy.

"Besides," said Grace, "not everyone is cut out for raising little ones. With the divorce rate today and all the problems with drugs and everything—well, I would count my lucky stars that I didn't have those worries. It takes a strong family to bring up a child right, and there aren't too many strong families these days." She looked to Tony for a response.

He polished off his cider and reached for more. "I wouldn't know," he said frankly. "My mother died when I was an infant, and my father brought me up— if you can call it that. I know as much about family life as I know about nuclear physics." He thought about the endless procession of nannies and prep schools and the loneliness he'd never admitted to.

"Surely your friends have married by now," Grace persisted. "Your brothers and sisters must have families."

"No brothers, no sisters," he said, aware of Jill's intense interest, "and most of my friends are into second and third marriages, not kids."

"Proves my point," said Grace. "Family life is an endangered species. Parenting is a lost art like stone carving. Shame, that, but true nonetheless."

Tony had never given much thought to parenting. Antony Graham Wellington III had also never given much thought to parenting—at least, not until his son, Tony, was old enough to walk and talk and graduate from Yale. A classic case of too little too late, and it had left Tony a stranger in a strange land when talk turned to the pleasures of having children.

How much pleasure could it involve if his own father, a pleasure-seeker of the first order, hadn't found time to explore it?

"Maybe that's for the best," he said out loud. "Maybe parenting should be left to the two or three people who can do it well."

"You sound cynical," Jill said, breaking her long silence. "Having a child is one of life's greatest gifts."

"So, how about you, Jill?" Grace asked before he could frame a response. "Any plans for a family?"

"Many plans," she said quietly. "None of which worked out." She looked like a Renaissance Madonna, a blend of such unexpected sorrow and beauty that he found it difficult to think.

He winced as Grace, oblivious of the haunted look in Jill's eyes, forged ahead. "Your husband didn't want a family?"

"Yes, he did," Jill said. "And he did a wonderful job starting one with another woman."

"You're better off without him," Grace said without batting an eyelash. "He wasn't one for the long haul."

Jill's eyes darted to his, and he held her gaze. *Nothing on earth could have made me leave you.*

Grace must have asked a question because he caught the words "tubal pregnancy" and "miscarriage."

Suddenly Jill pushed her chair back and stood up.

"Would you both excuse me? Your Steinway has been calling out to me, Grace, and if you don't mind, I'd love to play something."

With that, she disappeared down the hallway toward the front parlor.

"Did I say the wrong thing?" Grace asked.

"I don't know," Tony said.

Grace's eyes widened. "You mean you two aren't . . . ?"

He shook his head. "No," he said. "We aren't."

"Such a shame," said Grace. "We're not meant to go through this life alone."

"We're always alone," he said as the sounds of ragtime piano bounced into the country kitchen. "Nothing can change that."

"Poor boy." Grace patted his hand. "You really don't understand, do you?"

She got up to join Jill in the parlor and left Tony alone in the kitchen with the stone fireplace and the copper pots and the half century of love and trust and expectations.

If he had the guts, he'd storm into the parlor and sweep Jill into his arms. He'd carry her up the stairs to the bedroom at the end of the hall and he'd show her with his body all the things he could never say.

But, instead, he sat there for a long time with the dalmation on his lap, listening to the storm howling outside the window.

It was nothing compared to the storm inside his heart.

JILL AND THE BOLD CALICO had been curled up in the window seat for two hours, watching the snow falling. Actually, only Jill watched the snow fall; the kitten had the good sense to be asleep, cuddled in her arms.

Lucky cat.

Grace Benson's house echoed with forty-seven years of love. Every room, every corner, every photo on the mantelpiece, spoke of marriage the way it should be.

Not marriage the way she and Craig Wyatt had known it.

Archie and Grace Benson had managed to transcend time and temptation, illness and infertility, and forge a relationship that endured even now that Archie was gone. Like Jill's own parents, they'd faced reality then turned around and created their own particular heaven within it.

How she envied them.

How much she wanted to have that deep, abiding commitment with a man she could trust. A man she could rely on to be there when the going got tough.

A man like Tony Graham?

She laughed into the darkness. She'd heard Tony's opinions on marriage and family tonight. Family was an unknown quantity to him; marriage, something to be considered when he was too old to move on one more time. She'd heard it all, and each word had found its mark.

Why, then, did she still feel an emotional pull toward him that defied everything he said?

Why did she feel that they were somehow alike, each standing outside, looking in at the rest of the world?

Despite his wisecracks and his off-the-cuff remarks, she sensed a loneliness inside him that matched her own and she wished she had the courage to reach out to him.

The kitten on Jill's lap opened his eyes and looked up at her, his tiny paws stretching toward her. Jill gently touched the pink pads and laughed low.

"I know," she said. "Only a lunatic would still be up at this hour."

The kitten meowed then yawned, his teeth like tiny, ivory pinpoints in the soft darkness. It felt wonderful to hold him close, to feel his tiny heart beating. Why hadn't she realized how starved she was for the touch of something warm and alive?

Of how deeply she yearned to feel needed.

Maybe she'd become one of those determinedly single ladies with a houseful of cats and coupons for Kal-Kan taped to the refrigerator. At the moment, it sounded better than returning to her nothing life in Palm Beach.

"Come on, cutie." Jill stood up, holding the kitten in one hand and adjusting the belt on her robe with the other. "Let's go downstairs and raid the icebox."

Grace had given Jill and Tony carte blanche in the kitchen. Jill tiptoed past Tony's room, fighting back the urge to knock on his door and confront the tension that had been building between them.

Sublimate, she thought. *Sublimate.*

As she and the kitten, who was obviously her new best friend, went down the three flights of stairs to the kitchen, she turned her thoughts to the luscious blueberry pie she'd passed up earlier that evening.

"Idiot," she mumbled as she headed through the downstairs hallway.

Men were all as mercurial as the moody Mr. Graham.

A good blueberry pie was forever.

She pushed open the kitchen door and stopped in her tracks.

Well, at least it was forever until Tony got hold of it.

"Join the club," he said, motioning her to a chair at the huge oak kitchen table. "I finished the apple cobbler about an hour ago, but haven't reached the midway point on the blueberry. You're just in time."

"I didn't know you were a food freak," she said, putting her calico on the rocking chair next to his sibling and the dalmatian. "If you'd polished off that pie, I would have fired you on the spot."

"You forget something, ex-boss lady. I quit this afternoon."

She grabbed a plate from the cupboard over the sink and helped herself to a slice of epic proportions.

"Slipped my mind." She was determined to play it cool, despite the heat beginning to flood her body. "Didn't make coffee by any chance, did you?"

"Grace did. It's on the stove."

She filled her cup and sat down opposite him. "Where did you disappear to after dinner?" She took a sip of coffee. "My piano playing drive you out into the blizzard?"

"I've always been a sucker for a snowstorm."

She shivered and pulled her robe tight around her. "Snow belongs on ski slopes, not on the roads."

"Floridian blood," he said. "You need some toughening up."

"No, thanks." She looked at him, openly curious. "What were you doing out there?"

"Walking. Thinking. I tried to build a snowman but it's not good packing snow."

"Packing snow?"

"Forget it, Palm Beach. It's too esoteric a concept for you."

She shook her head. "There you go again. What truck driver on earth would use the word 'esoteric' in casual conversation?"

"Ex-truck driver."

She broke off a piece of pie with her fork. "I hear there's a job opening in Fire Creek," she said, keeping her expression neutral. "A traveling piano player could use some help."

"I've heard about those traveling piano players," he said, his own expression equally bland. "Tough to work for."

"Not this one. She minds her own business, let's the driver call his own shots."

"Definitely atypical."

"Interested?"

"Could be." He met her eyes across the table. "You hiring?"

She didn't look away. "Could be."

"I'm a good driver," he said. "My last boss thought highly of me."

She laughed into her coffee cup. "*You* were your last boss, Graham. That's hardly a recommendation."

"You should have thought of that the first time you hired me."

She extended her right hand to him across the table. "Deal?"

He took her hand in his and a warm feeling moved through her body. "Deal."

They shook solemnly. She moved to break the contact but his grip shifted until they were holding hands as something other than business partners. All the unfocused feelings she'd had that night rushed in at her at once.

She swallowed. "So you're back on the payroll again."

"Not yet."

A heaviness flooded her stomach and thighs at the intimate sound of his voice. "Not yet?" she repeated.

"Tomorrow morning." He turned her hand over and traced a pattern along her wrist with his thumb. "Tomorrow morning I'll do whatever you want."

"And tonight?" Her voice was barely a whisper in the quiet kitchen.

"Tonight belongs to us." He rose, still holding her hand, then moved closer to where she sat. "Stand up, Jill."

She hesitated, uncertain her legs could support her weight. Tony seemed to sense her problem and, smiling slightly, he took her other hand, and she stood. Gently, he tilted her chin until her eyes met his.

"This isn't what I was expecting when I hired you," she managed, her voice soft with longing.

He drew his thumb gently across the fullness of her lower lip. "This isn't what I expected when I took the job." He dipped his head and brushed his mouth against hers. "It's what I wanted."

"So did I," she whispered. "From the first moment I saw you."

"Come upstairs with me," he said softly. "It's more than time."

"Yes," she whispered, resting her forehead against his shoulder. "It is, isn't it?"

The longing that had begun the second they met crystallized, and she wondered how she ever could have doubted they would one day reach this moment.

Her hands rested lightly at his waist. The heat from his body sizzled through his light sweater and singed her fingertips. The urge to push past barriers was too strong to resist, and she let her hands slide under his sweater and rest along the smooth, taut ridge of muscle above the waistband of his faded jeans.

"You don't know how many times I dreamed of doing this," she murmured against his lips.

"You should have said something." His sweet breath against her skin made her tremble with pleasure. "I wouldn't have minded."

"Sexual harassment." She caught his lower lip between her teeth and savored its fullness for just a moment. "A boss can't be too careful."

His hands traveled down her back until he lightly cupped her buttocks and drew her closer to his strength.

"Don't be careful, Jill." His voice was deep, seductive. Thrilling. "Tonight be anything you want."

She traced her nails lightly across the muscles of his back and laughed low in her throat at the delicious power she had over him. A woman's power—a vital force she'd long forgotten. But that power flooded her now, bringing with it magic and mystery and a sweet, sweet desire that made everything but this moment—and this man—disappear like a sorcerer's dream.

"Anything I want?" No coyness. No flirtation. They had traveled too far for that.

He nodded. A vein near his right temple throbbed noticeably. "Anything you want."

"You," she said, knowing from that moment there'd be no turning back. "It's you I want."

He brought his mouth to hers—or did she move into his kiss?

It hardly mattered.

As soon as their lips touched, as soon as their breaths mingled and her mouth opened to receive him, nothing at all mattered but this dizzying, glorious swirl of sensual pleasure that swept them up into another world.

Arm in arm, they climbed the first two flights of steps, then, on the landing, he swept her into his arms and carried her to her third-floor room.

"Very romantic," she murmured against his ear, "but why not all three flights?"

His chuckle rumbled against her skin. "Because I want strength for more important things."

And then they were in her room with its crazy-angled ceiling and huge four-poster bed and the window that looked out onto the snow and the shimmering silver moon. The last of Jill's fears surfaced as he lowered her onto the bed.

"It's been a long time for me," she said, meeting Tony's eyes. "I may not be all that you expect." She'd heard enough of his conversation with Grace that evening to know his approach to love was much different than hers. He seemed to embody the eighties, while Jill sometimes felt herself a throwback to an older, more serious time.

He said nothing, just watched her, those beautiful green eyes of his shadowed with an emotion she couldn't quite grasp. What a ridiculous, naive fool of a woman she must seem to him.

"So much for fun and games," she said, suddenly embarrassed. She tried to slide away but he neatly blocked her with his body. "Maybe you should drive back and look for our friend Taffy. Maybe she could—"

He pulled her down next to him on the bed until she lay on her side, facing him. "This is the woman I want to make love to." He brought his hand down on her hip and slowly drew it across her belly, her rib cage, until it closed around her breast. "There's no one else in this bed, Jill. If you believe nothing else, believe that."

"I've been with just one man," she said, determined to make him understand. "I don't know the rules. I—"

But then there were no more rules, no more words, no more thoughts; there was nothing beyond the way his mouth felt as it covered hers, the way his breath, fragrant with apples and hot coffee, made her dizzy with longing, the way his body pressed against her own and drove her to move against him in a way she'd thought long forgotten.

Her fingers, so sure, so graceful at the piano, fumbled with the buttons on his shirt in her eagerness to feel the warmth of his skin against her own. He parted her robe, and it slid down over her shoulders, exposing her breasts. The night air was chill, and she shivered slightly but then she bared his chest and he flung his shirt somewhere into the darkness and his heat quickly became her own.

A sound, low and new, built in her throat, surprising her with its intensity.

"Don't hold back," he said, leaning over her, all male dominance and beauty. "Don't ever hold back with me. I want it all, Jill. Everything you have."

He lowered his head and drew her nipple into his mouth, that hot wet secret place that seemed to be drawing her soul away from her body and replacing it with something wild and free and wonderful.

Something she hadn't known before.

The cry of pleasure she'd been fighting back broke free, and Tony once again covered her mouth with his, absorbing the sound and the passion that had prompted it.

The rest of their clothing became barriers to be torn down, and quickly they each stripped off their garments, then faced each other with nothing separating them but these long, exquisite moments of expectation.

She leaned back against the huge goosedown pillows, trying to control the desire to cover herself as his gaze flamed across her naked body. Nothing escaped his eyes or the raging fire that coiled its way throughout her body.

He was beautifully made, as she had known he would be. His body, backlit by the moon outside the window, was strong and lithe and undeniably ready for her. She knew that the sight of him as he knelt over her—his

need for her so blatant, so honest, so miraculous—
would stay with her beyond this night.

She raised her arms toward him, a gesture of both
submission and demand. He grabbed her wrists with
one hand then brought her fingers to his mouth, caressing each with his tongue until she was certain she
would implode with passion denied.

"Tony," she said, yearning for him. "Please...
now..."

He nipped at her wrist, his mouth pressed to her pulse
point. "Just wait," he said, reaching for his pants,
which lay on the floor beside the bed. "Let me take care
of something."

Instantly she knew what he meant. "You don't need
it."

His silence filled the room. "You're on the Pill?" He
sounded uncertain.

She didn't want to begin the relationship with a lie.
"No." She took a deep breath then laid her heart bare.
"I can't have children."

He hesitated then she heard the slither as his jeans fell
to the floor.

"Jill," he said, his voice softer, more caring than
she'd ever heard it. "Are you sure?"

Her laugh was shaky but she was in control. "Oh,
yes." She thought of her visit to Doctor Beauman a few
days ago. "I'm hale and hearty and definitely sterile."

The falling snow outside was the loudest sound in the
room.

"Tony," she said. "Did you hear me?"

His arms slid around her, his large hands warm
against the small of her back.

"I heard you, but it doesn't change a thing."

"Really?"

"Really."

He pressed a kiss against the hollow of her belly. "Come to me, Jill."

Something in Jill broke free then, the wild and passionate spirit that had been fenced in for so long.

She rested her face against his neck and inhaled deeply, letting her fingertips explore the muscles of his chest, the flat planes of his belly and beyond.

I love you, she thought.

God help her, but she'd fallen in love.

Chapter Eleven

It wasn't until darkness vanished with the dawn that they finally found what they'd been searching for: that shattering second of realization that nothing between them would ever be the same again.

There had been no holding back between them. Physically, they had created pleasures Jill had only dreamed of. Emotionally, they had taken chances sane people—people not in the grip of love—wouldn't dare consider.

But then there was nothing sane, nothing safe, about the way Tony Graham made her feel. She was as wild and free and beautiful as the land they'd grown to love.

"It stopped snowing," Tony murmured lazily as their spirits floated back down to earth.

Jill leaned up on one elbow and looked toward the window. Daylight outlined the snow-covered trees and buildings outside with a pale lemon glow. "You're very observant. I'm duly impressed."

He pulled her back down next to him. "What I am, is hungry."

"Tony! After all we've—"

"Sorry to disappoint you, boss lady, but it's the blueberry pie I've been thinking about."

"Since we're telling the truth, I've been fantasizing about the same thing." She threw back the covers and made to leave, but he held her fast. "Come on." She tugged at his arm. "When it comes to food, I take no prisoners."

"Wait a minute, Jill," he said, his voice oddly controlled. "There's something I want to talk about, and this seems as good a time as any."

Instantly she went as cold and hard as the ground outside.

Don't let me cry, she warned herself. Whatever he said, however he broached the inevitable, she wasn't going to let it show.

She waited silently, poised for flight.

He met her eyes. "My name's not Tony Graham."

Maybe he wasn't speaking English. "What did you say?"

"I said, my name's not Tony Graham." He ran a hand through his tousled hair. "It's not really as bad as it sounds. Actually I am Tony Graham in a way—Antony Graham Wellington IV."

She stared at him. Her truck driver? Her blue-collar fantasy man?

Her lover?

"Tony IV?" she managed. If he'd said Tony the Tiger, she couldn't have been more surprised.

"Pretty awful, isn't it?"

"And Graham is your middle name?"

"Guilty."

There was no time like the present.

"Well, surprise, Tony IV: Wiley is really *my* middle name." She extended her right hand. "Mr. Welles—"

"Wellington."

"Mr. Wellington, meet Jillian Wiley Kathryn Von Eron—the first."

His eyes widened the way they had the day she nearly drove over the cliff on the way to Devil's Heart. "Von Eron?"

"Yep."

"The Von Erons who own Tri-Mutual Finance and the Liberty Building in Manhattan and most of Rhode Island?"

She nodded. "And a good chunk of Palm Beach. You can see why I used my middle name." To an unscrupulous type, the Von Eron name would represent a ticket to the easy life.

Tony started to laugh. "Why do you think I used Graham?" he countered. "What your family doesn't own, my family does."

He named four multinational corporations and a well-known foundation. Jill whistled. "I see what you mean." She wrapped the quilt around her bare shoulders and leaned back against the brass headboards. "Which leads me to my next question: What on earth are you doing driving a truck?"

He leaned back against the headboard next to her. "Beats the hell out of me."

She poked him in the stomach. "Get serious, friend. You don't find many multimillionaires playing piano mover."

"No," he said dryly. "Most multimillionaires are bums."

She poked him again. "I resent that! Pa and my father work harder than anyone I know."

"Anomalies." He told her about the crazy bet he and his father had made.

"So this cost you a Rolls Royce, did it?" She drew her fingernail lightly across his flat belly and grinned at his amazing reaction.

He rolled her over onto her back and pinned her hands over her head. "I don't give a damn if it cost three Rolls Royces."

She started to laugh as he did strangely wonderful things to her breasts with his mouth.

"You have me at an unfair advantage," she said, not struggling at all as he gently tugged at one diamond-hard nipple.

"Any complaints?" His eyes glittered with a wild passion that matched her own.

But it wasn't passion that consumed her at the moment—it was curiosity. She finally wriggled out of his grip and pulled the sheet over her breasts.

"At least now I can guess where you got your vocabulary from. Princeton? Dartmouth?"

"Yale—although they may not want to claim me as an alumnus."

"Truck driving's an honorable way to make a living."

"It's not the truck driving that would bother them; it's the fact that I was a bum for the twenty-eight years before it."

"A bum?"

"A bum."

"You must have done something, Tony."

He shook his head.

"I don't believe it. Not with all those companies your father owns." She knew from both her father and her grandfather that there was an endless amount of work connected with running huge corporations. Enough work to employ every member of a huge family—that is, if they wanted to be employed.

"Sorry to disillusion you, boss lady. I took the easy road."

"Wait a minute!" Her mind zoomed back to their first meeting. "What about the top-secret trucking firm you mentioned at your interview? I suppose that was fictitious?"

He put his arms behind his head. "The company was real," he admitted. "I'm the one who wasn't. I ran it into the red in six months."

"But you're so good at organization," she said. "Look at what you've done for me." Hank's help had only been preliminary; Tony had made it all work.

"That's not organization," he said. "That's motivation."

"Motivation?"

He took her hand and kissed her palm, then folded her fingers one by one over the spot where his lips had been.

"Seems pretty simple to me. I did it for you."

Her heart tightened with a sweet pain. "I still don't understand."

"I think you do." He touched her hair, her cheek, her lips with his forefinger. "I'm in love with you, Jill."

She ducked her head for an instant and tried to control the joy his words brought with them. "That's what I hoped you meant."

"Want me to say it again?" His forefinger trailed down her throat and traced the angle of her collarbone. Who would have imagined the collarbone a source of such delight? "I'm in love with you, Jill."

She blinked once, twice, to clear her vision. Those were words she'd never expected to hear, words hidden away in her deepest fantasies. Words to hold close for a lifetime, however long that lifetime might last. "I was afraid I was the only one," she said. "I fell in love with you in Branchwater."

"That night by the swimming pool."

Memories of how he'd looked in the moonlight made it difficult to think. "I'd never had a moment of such pure happiness before."

"Maybe it was the moonlight," he said, reading her mind. "Or the music. Maybe—"

She silenced him with a kiss. "It was you, Tony. It was having you to share it with that made it so special." Take away the moonlight and the music; take away the audience and the adulation and it wouldn't matter a damn.

She'd still have the joy she'd felt from Tony, from laughing with him, and yes, fighting with him. Loving him had been a natural progression, one as inevitable as a heartbeat.

"I saw a for-sale sign in Grace's front window," he said. "How would you feel about telling the rest of the world to go to hell and living in Fire Creek forever?"

"Right now it sounds like paradise on earth."

"You love this state, don't you?"

She nodded. "There's something magical about it," she said. "All my life I've felt a connection."

He ruffled her hair. "You're so much like your grandfather. That's how you said he felt about his ranch."

"Amazing, isn't it? Sometimes I think I got it by osmosis."

"I think heredity had something to do with it."

"Not in this case, Tony. I'm adopted."

He turned slightly and looked at her. "I didn't know."

"How could you? It never came up before." She told him about her mother, the former Aggie Wiley, about Aggie and Hank's famous fights, about her parents and the love-at-first-sight romance that had been going strong for almost thirty years. And then she decided to make a conscious leap of faith and sketched in the story of her marriage—and her miscarriage.

"I want you to understand one thing: no babies, Tony. No little Tony V with his daddy's dimple. It's not going to happen, no matter how much I want it."

"I don't have a dimple," he said, his grin obliterating his argument.

She refused to be sidetracked. "You know what I'm saying. I lost my husband because I can't get pregnant. If it's going to be a problem, say so now. Let me know where I stand."

He reached for her but she slid toward the edge of the bed.

"You're proof that adoptions work, aren't you?" he asked.

"You're still avoiding the issue."

He stopped smiling. "You want it straight?"

"I want it straight."

"I'm not looking to become a father, Jill. It's not something I want. It never has been."

"Then you're in the minority. Most men want a junior version."

"I'm what happens when a man gets his junior version and doesn't know what to do with him." He pushed his hair off his forehead with a swift, sharp gesture that told Jill they were in dangerous territory.

"You may not always feel that way, Tony." Why did she feel this insane urge to push? She wanted to broach the topic of adoption again, but he raised his hand to stop her. "Things change."

"Not this." He told her about his father, about their volatile relationship and the years it had taken Tony to resign himself to the fact that what was, was probably all there'd ever be. "Kids?" he said, looking off toward the window. "No, thanks."

There was no uncertainty in his voice, no hidden longings to leap out at her one day and destroy what they had.

He pulled her down across his lap and cupped her chin. His palm was rough, his fingertips newly callused from work. Desires she'd believed well satisfied reappeared, full-blown.

"I want you, Jill, not what you can give me. I can't make it any simpler than that." The look in his eyes blasted away the last of her fears.

"Tony." She wrapped her arms around his neck and moved closer until his face was just inches from hers.

"What, boss lady?"

"Shut up."

They didn't talk again for a very long time.

NOTHING IN TONY'S LIFE had prepared him for the wonder of Jill Wiley.

Correction: Jillian Von Eron.

He felt as if he'd traveled one hundred years in just twenty-four hours. The image he'd had of himself as a loner, someone meant to travel through the rest of his life the way he'd traveled through the first twenty-eight years of it, had been blown to bits the moment he took her into his arms.

That morning they'd bundled up and gone for a walk in the snow, and Tony felt closer to being in a state of grace than he had at any other time of his life. She understood play, Jill did, in a way that freed the child in him. They built a snowman and tied a Hermes scarf around its neck. She shared his ironic amusement over the rites and privileges of "old money," and when he added his Diner's Club card to the picture, she burst into applause.

They traded both snowballs and stories as they roamed the woods behind Grace's house.

He was surprised the snow didn't melt in his hands because the love he felt for her burned inside him.

She'd been so strong, so fiercely independent and honest, when she told him she couldn't have children that he'd wanted to reach inside her heart and take away the pain that loss had caused her.

She was enough. What they had together was more than he'd thought to have in his lifetime. Miraculously it had taken stepping out of his own life to find a woman who understood the pain and pleasure inherent in great privilege, one who was willing to build a life that followed only the rules of her heart.

The truth was, he felt married to her already. They were mirror images finally come together. What they'd discovered last night in that big four-poster bed had only confirmed all that went before.

Everything he wanted, everything he needed, was there in that tiny town, in the arms of Jillian Wiley Von Eron.

If he had his way, he'd buy Grace's house and Fire Creek, Nevada—and maybe Devil's Heart and Paiute Hollow, for good measure—and live there with her forever.

But, by midafternoon the roads around Fire Creek were cleared of snow, and the truck was warmed up, and there they were, saying goodbye to Grace Benson and her menagerie.

Tony had already said goodbye and he stood by the truck, waiting. Women were a mysterious sex. Why say goodbye once when a thousand times would do?

Jill and Grace hugged each other again while the two calico cats played in the snow at their feet. The Labrador had had sense enough to stay indoors, and the puppy's face could be seen peeping out the window of the front parlor.

"Now you two make sure you stop back here from time to time," said Grace as they trooped over to Tony. "My door is always open."

He couldn't resist giving Grace another goodbye hug himself. "We will," he said, meaning it. "You can bet on it."

Grace reached up and rubbed at his cheek with her thumb. "Lipstick," she said with a wink. "Not my color."

Tony cast a quick look at Jill, but she was occupied with the kitten who had tangled his paw in her hoop earring.

"Oh, don't you worry about being embarrassed," Grace said, her voice low. "If ever I saw two young people in love, it was you two."

"We weren't certain until last night," he said, amazed that he could speak so freely with someone he barely knew. "I think it was your blueberry pie that did it."

Grace threw her head back and was laughing heartily as Jill, kitten in her arms, walked up to them.

"What's the joke, you two?"

"Blueberry pie," said Grace. "The wonders of."

Tony didn't elaborate any further. Jill looked from Grace to him then shrugged.

"Go ahead," she said. "Have your secrets. I'm more interested in this little guy anyway." She scratched the kitten behind the ear one last time then handed him back to Grace. "You and your sister better be good. No scratching the furniture."

"Might as well tell a bird not to fly," Grace said. "Cats scratch furniture and that's just the way it is."

"We'd better hit the road," Tony said at last. "We have a lot of miles to cover before dark."

"Wait a minute!" Grace's voice stopped them just as he opened the passenger door. She scooped up both kittens. "Here," she said to Jill. "They're yours."

Jill laughed in delight. "I couldn't."

I agree, he thought. They'd be swinging from the suspension system and using the Bornsdorfer as a giant litter box.

"Sure you could," said Grace. He'd once believed her to be a very bright woman. "They've been back and forth to Reno with me. They're as adaptable as kids."

Jill was already up to her eyebrows in cat fur. "What do you think?" she asked him.

"How happy are they going to be in the back of a truck?"

"I didn't think they'd be in the back."

"You weren't thinking about the front seat, were you?"

"Guilty. My lap, actually."

"What about when we're eating? Sleeping? What about when you're performing? Are you going to leave them locked in the truck?"

"I hadn't thought that far ahead." She nuzzled the neck of the larger kitten. "It wouldn't be fair, would it?"

He didn't say anything.

Jill handed the kittens back to Grace. "I wish I could," she said. "Thank you for the offer."

"Animals are like kids," Grace said, repeating her earlier analogy. "They're a big responsibility. Better not to take them if you can't give them what they need."

How right you are, Grace.

Someone should have told Antony III the same thing twenty-eight years ago.

"YOU KNOW I WAS RIGHT about the cats," Tony said when they were some fifty miles past Fire Creek. "They never would have been happy cooped up in this truck."

"I know," Jill said for the third time since they pulled out of Grace's driveway. He seemed unable to let the subject drop. "You were one hundred percent right. It would never have worked." She turned her attention to the itinerary he'd been working on while she was back in Palm Beach seeing Hank. "Two shows in Mirror Lake? How did you manage that?"

"If you want those kittens, we could turn around."

And they said women were changeable. She let her head drop back against her seat and groaned. "Enough talk about those kittens, Tony, please! Yes, I fell in love with them. Yes, I would have taken them in a second. But, no, I don't want to change my mind. They need more stability than we can give them in the back of a truck. Now will you please let it drop?"

He started to say something, and she raised her hand.

"One more apology and I swear I'll walk the rest of the way to Devil's Heart. I think I liked you better when we argued all the time."

He glanced over at her, that wonderful twinkle back in his green eyes. "I think I liked you better last night when..." He recounted one of her own particular favorite moments.

"You have a wonderful way with a story, Graham," she said, pretending to inspect her manicure. "Tell me another one."

He did. It was even better than the first.

"You realize these are bedtime stories, don't you?" he asked.

"I had that feeling," she said. "Maybe you should save a few for later."

"What a boss." He looked over at her and started to laugh. "Hell," he said. "What a woman!"

AND SO IT WENT.

For the next three weeks they argued and laughed and loved their way through northern Nevada. Spring had finally come to stay, and wildflowers in shades of yellow and red and blue stretched from horizon to horizon.

Tony could infuriate her with a word; he could make her burn for him with a glance; but what he did the very best was make her laugh. She couldn't remember a time when she'd felt so filled with happiness, so optimistic. So sure her life was going in the right direction—and that she had finally found the right man.

And, if that weren't enough, this crazy idea to take her Juilliard training and her grand piano and hit the road had turned out to be one of the best things she'd ever done.

For a self-proclaimed professional "bum," Antony Graham Wellington IV was one brilliant manager. He'd found the only electronics store in Devil's Heart and bought a laptop computer. Two days later he'd set up a data base that catalogued distances, points of contact and all the piano tuners from Reno to Las Vegas.

At every one of their stops he made endless phone calls that invariably led to more opportunities for Jill to play everything from Bach to Beethoven to the Boss.

The possibilities seemed endless but, as it was, she was finding the pace they were keeping to be surprisingly exhausting. Maybe it was the cool mountain air or the huge meals they always managed to devour—or maybe it was just the novelty of having something to fill every moment, but she found herself dropping off to sleep in the passenger's seat so often that she finally bought herself a pillow at a J. C. Penney in Stone City and napped in comfort.

She was taking one of those luxurious naps in the middle of their fourth week out when Tony kissed her awake in a Mcdonald's parking lot and said, "We're lost."

"Not again." She pushed her face deeper into the pillow. "I thought you and your computer had everything under control."

He gave her a swat on the bottom. "My navigator's been sleeping on the job."

"I'm the boss," she mumbled. "Not the navigator."

"I needed someone to read the map."

"Hire someone," she said, giving up on sleep. "You can afford it."

"Not on what you're paying me."

"You're rich," she shot back. "Use your trust fund."

He lunged for her, and she flung open the door and leaped out, getting a good ten-yard head start as she dashed across the blacktop parking lot.

"Big Mac and large fries," she called out as she raced inside and headed for the ladies' room, the last bastion of privacy left to womankind. "And don't forget the chocolate shake."

Once safely in the rest room, she bent over the sink and splashed cold water on her face, then searched in vain for some paper towels. It was either her T-shirt or the hot-air blower attached to the wall at munchkin level. Considering the fact they desperately needed to find a Laundromat and a dry cleaner, she opted for the blower.

Angling it up the best she could, Jill bent down in front of the blast of hot, dry air, then caught a glimpse of herself in the mirror. Her bangs stuck up in tufts. Her ponytail drooped. Her face was totally bare of make-up.

It must be love, she thought as she tried to comb her hair with her fingers. Either that or Tony was totally insane.

Her old society pals from Palm Beach would never recognize her. She laughed out loud. Her own mother would never recognize her. She could just imagine Agneta's horror if she knew her daughter ventured forth each day without eye cream and SPF 15.

And how totally, wonderfully crazy it was that she'd had to travel so far to find a man who not only shared her privileged background, but her own out-of-synch disrespect for all the nonsense it represented.

There'd always been too much of Hank's soul in Jill to enable her to look at corporate politics and big business shenanigans with anything but amusement. A life of ladies' teas and hospital fund-raisers would have been a slow death.

Tony was the man she'd never believed existed, the man fate had intended her to find.

If she'd ever had any doubts about lucky stars and four-leaf clovers and wishing on a rainbow, she didn't have them any longer.

Short of a full twelve hours' sleep, she had everything she wanted.

She pushed open the bathroom door and found Tony juggling two trays piled high with food.

"Don't just look at me," he groaned the second he caught sight of her. "Give me a hand!"

She grabbed one of the trays and followed him outside to a picnic table by a grove of pine trees.

Oh, yes, she thought. She definitely had everything she wanted.

How terrific that she was smart enough to know it this time around.

THEY ATE IN COMPANIONABLE SILENCE, broken only by occasional comments on how you could get away from civilization, but you could never get away from the golden arches, which made Jill feel especially guilty since her grandfather owned a rival fast-food chain.

Tony asked the counter clerk with the carrot-red hair about public telephones, and she directed them two miles down the road.

Jill had to hand it to him; he checked and double-checked everything, even to the point of calling ahead and reconfirming sleeping arrangements and help with the piano. Jill tried to call home every four or five days to make certain Hank was okay. She grabbed the phone next to Tony and punched in the numbers.

"Is Pa all right?" she asked the second she heard her mother's breathless, frazzled greeting. "What's going on?"

"He did it again! That man did it again."

Her entire body stiffened. "Did what?" *Please, God, not another heart attack.*

"He's getting married again, that's what! He and that Mary Small have decided to become engaged. Is there no end to that man's foolishness?"

Anxiety instantly turned into delight. "I knew it!" she crowed, drawing Tony's attention. "The minute I met Mary I knew she was the one."

"Well, I wish you'd told me your suspicions, darling," her mother huffed. "There you are in the middle of nowhere, and I'm here trying to gather myself together and plan a party—"

"Back up, Mother. Plan what party?"

"Their engagement party, of course."

"You swore after his fourth marriage that you'd never throw another engagement party for Pa, no matter how many fiancées he brought back."

"You're much too literal," said her mother. "You take after your father. Well, of course we're going to have a party for your grandfather. Whatever would Mary think of us if we let this occasion pass by without the proper festivities?"

"Mary is sixty-eight years old, Mother. She'd probably just as soon elope."

Agneta was not about to be swayed. "The party will be two weeks from tomorrow, and I trust you'll be home in time to join us."

As if anything could keep her away. She glanced over at Tony who was finishing up his own conversation and eyeing Jill curiously. It might also be the perfect opportunity to introduce him to the rest of her family.

"I'll be there," she promised. "Wild horses couldn't keep me away."

Agneta was well past rationality and she wouldn't let Jill go until she promised to get back at least three or four days before the party "just in case."

In case of what was still unclear even after Jill hung up but, then, her mother had always been a beloved mystery.

"You'll never believe it," she said to Tony as they walked back to the truck. "Pa's getting married again."

Tony threw his head back and laughed. "All right! The old man just doesn't slow down, does he?"

"You don't know the half of it."

As they headed toward Fox Creek she sketched in the highlights of Hank's exploits with the opposite sex.

"Five times?" Tony whistled. "He doesn't believe in learning by his own mistakes, does he?"

"He doesn't think he's made any mistakes."

"Four divorces mean something, Jill."

"Not to Pa. He's a hopeless romantic." She looked over at him. "It runs in the family. We all absolutely refuse to believe in anything less than a happy ending."

"Funny thing, boss lady," he said, meeting her eyes. "I'm beginning to feel the same way."

EIGHT DAYS LATER they were back at the airport once again.

Jill was waiting for Hank's private jet to taxi in while Tony's Wellington-family plane was due within the hour.

"Are you sure I can't change your mind?" she asked as the Wiley jet came into view. "If there's anything my mother loves, it's houseguests."

He shook his head. "I'll be there for the party, Jill, I promise."

"Can't convince you?"

"Can't convince me. I have some loose ends to take care of and this is as good a time as any."

She wrapped her arms around his waist. "I'm going to miss you."

He kissed her deeply. "That's what I like to hear."

"I wish we could go back to Fire Creek and buy Grace's house."

"It's all possible, Jill," he said. "There's nothing we can't do."

Hank's pilot, Jerry, popped up next to her. "Ready when you are, miss," he said, nodding at Tony.

"Friday?" she asked, kissing him one more time.

"Friday," he said, walking her to the opening to the jetway. "You have my word."

LOOSE ENDS, she thought an hour later as the jet crossed over the Kansas plains. What loose ends could he be talking about?

They were coming closer and closer to making a real commitment and, deep down, she knew these loose ends were more important than just getting his father that Rolls Royce. What they'd found together was a lasting kind of love, and the subject of marriage was imminent. The kind that made talk of wonderful old Victorian houses more fraught with meaning than just a discussion of real estate.

Their courtship had been those crazy days and nights on the road, dragging the Bornsdorfer from Branchwater to Paiute Hollow to Duck Tail. Laughing and fighting and working together, they'd seen the best and the worst each had to offer, and love had bloomed along with the spring flowers on the mountainside.

Making love had been a true consummation of all that came before, a joining of their souls as well as their bodies in a way she knew bound them together forever.

Whatever his "loose ends" were, she wasn't going to worry about them. Not when she had a more pressing problem on her mind: how to introduce Tony to her parents.

"Boyfriend" sounded too high school. "Lover" was too personal while "significant other" sounded like some Yuppie hybrid dreamed up by *Cosmo* and *Ms*.

Besides, her mother would know the minute she saw her that something momentous had happened.

She curled up in her seat.

Loose ends?

There were a thousand of them.

She yawned and closed her eyes.

It was all too confusing and she was so tired. . . .

MANHATTAN
Three days later

"TO THE VICTOR BELONGS THE SPOILS." Tony tossed his father the keys to a brand-new shiny, black Rolls Royce. "Enjoy."

Antony Graham Wellington III opened the driver's door and climbed inside. "No grumbling about unfair odds? No apologies for underestimating the idle rich?"

"None," said Tony as he climbed into the huge car next to him. "You won fair and square."

His father turned the key, and the engine sprang to life instantly.

"You've changed," Wellington the elder said as he maneuvered the car through the crowded private garage of the Emory Club. "I can't put my finger on it, but you've changed. Did your brush with reality bring you back to your senses?"

Yes. I've discovered there's more to life than you would ever guess, Dad. Let me tell you about her.

But, as usual, he didn't. Instead he slumped lower in his seat as the car plowed into the maze of Manhattan traffic. "My brush with reality, as you put it, was the best damned thing that ever happened to me."

"A cryptic statement. Care to elaborate?"

I'm in love, Dad. I'm going to ask her to marry me.

How could he explain to this stranger who was his father everything he had discovered out there on the road in Nevada? How could a man wedded to the bottom line of a stock report understand anything of the freedom and wonder Tony had found with Jill Von Eron?

So Tony did what he did best: backed away from it. He leaned over and flipped on the radio hidden in a chunk of highly polished wood. "Let's check out the sound system."

"Fine," said his father, turning toward Riverside Drive. "Let's."

By THE TIME TONY GOT BACK to his apartment later on, he wanted nothing more than a Scotch and a good night's sleep.

It had been a hell of a day.

Why had he ever thought things could be different between his father and him? More than age distanced them—years of traveling in opposite directions had taken them so far away from each other that his chances of becoming governor of Nevada were greater than his chances of ever understanding what made his father tick.

He poured himself a drink and stretched out on his couch, his shoes scattering dirt over the pale silk upholstery. The old loneliness that had been with him from the time he was old enough to recognize it for what it was swept down, and he realized how many changes Jill had brought into his life.

It all, always and forever, came back to Jill.

She was living proof of the unimportance of blood ties, the feminine counterpart of her passionate, life-loving grandfather—a living, breathing embodiment of everything wonderful about Hank Wiley.

Tony grinned.

And some not-so-wonderful things as well.

Yet she was adopted. Hank's blood didn't flow through her veins. The genetic codes of the Wileys and Von Erons had played no part in the woman she'd become.

Of course, that shouldn't surprise him. He shared his father's blood and bone, yet the only thing they truly had in common was the illustrious Wellington name.

His connection with Jill was stronger than anything he'd ever known, the most powerful, joyous experience of his life.

Responsibility had never been his strong suit; commitment, never his forte. With Jill it was all different. He was ready now to forge that lasting bond.

He'd felt her pain, sharp and swift, when she told him about her sterility but a part of him was glad there would be no Wellington V. It was hardly surprising he had such a lousy view of parenthood: He'd spent twenty-eight years trying to gain his father's approval and he'd be damned if he'd do that to any kid of his.

He and Jill were lucky to be young and healthy and rich beyond most people's wildest dreams. They had everything they needed to build a life of incredible happiness, and that's exactly what he intended them to do. There was a whole world out there to explore together. He had countless ideas for what he'd dubbed Mozart-to-Go, ideas that could translate into an operation spreading throughout rural and back-country America. Hell, Alaska would probably jump at the idea, too.

They could go as far as their imaginations and love could carry them.

Just the two of them.

He finished his drink and looked out the window at the shimmering lights of Tavern on the Green in the distance.

But what he owed her was a fresh start.

Tomorrow morning he would wipe the slate clean, sever his ties with Denise and Rafaela and Jennifer and all the other women he'd managed to woo then walk away from, relying on charm to keep his options open long after he'd found someone else.

He'd prided himself on his sense of style; he never broke a woman's heart when he moved on. No harsh words. No scenes.

No goodbyes.

Especially no goodbyes.

Now he saw it for what it was: A way to avoid any real commitment, to keep his heart out of danger, to skim the surface of life by taking the pleasure and avoiding the deeper joys only risk could provide.

By keeping his options open he was closing the door to the real thing.

No more.

When he went down to Palm Beach for the old man's engagement party, he would go free of entanglements, free of old relationships, free of everything but this love he had for her, and then, beneath the palm trees, he would ask Jillian Wiley Kathryn Von Eron to marry him.

And he wouldn't leave until she said yes.

PALM BEACH
Three days later

JILL WAS STRETCHED OUT on a float in the outdoor pool, eyes closed behind her sunglasses, trying to ignore the waves of fatigue lapping all around her.

For days she'd done little but sleep. Twelve-, fourteen-, sixteen-hour stretches of deep, dreamless sleep that left her groggy and disoriented but still as exhausted as before.

At first she'd blamed it on those crazy days on the road, on the incredible pace they'd been keeping, but obviously she'd been wrong. It was six days since she'd arrived in Palm and, if anything, she was more tired than before.

Other than the way she missed Tony, the only thing in her life was her overwhelming need for sleep.

Agneta had been aiming a few pointed remarks about her narcoleptic behavior in Jill's direction that she'd so far managed to deflect, and she'd been aware of the concern on her father's face at dinner the night she almost fell asleep with her face in the consommé.

Although she didn't let on, this dreadful fatigue was beginning to frighten her. Instead of lessening, it seemed to take over a bit more of her with every new day. Her appetite was gone; her energy depleted. She felt as if she were up against an unseen enemy who was systematically draining her ounce by ounce of all her vitality.

The notion that something could be seriously wrong with her was beginning to work its way into her brain with increasing regularity, and she didn't like it. Not one bit.

Thank God, the house was in an uproar with preparations for the engagement party. Hank and Mary were flying down tonight in his Lear and, from her last chat with her future step-grandmother, the two of them were as excited about the party as a young couple embarking on the sea of matrimony for the very first time.

If she weren't so tired, Jill would send up a cheer for young lovers of all ages.

Today the house was a whirl of caterers and florists and cleaning people, and it had been easy to slip out the back door and give herself up to the sun and the easy, lulling peace of the swimming pool.

A gentle breeze curled itself around her, and she was about to drift off into sleep when her mother's voice pulled her back.

"If you're that tired, darling, why don't you go back to bed?"

"I'm not that tired, Mother. I'm working on my tan."

"You never tan; you burn, and you're already working up a lovely shade of scarlet. At least use some sunblock."

"I bet George Hamilton's mother doesn't tell him to use sunblock." The perpetually tanned actor had probably been born a shade of burnished walnut.

"George Hamilton's not a blonde."

Jill heard her mother's footsteps round the northern edge of the pool and head in her direction. She let her hands dangle into the water and tried to casually propel herself out of reach but Agneta was too sharp for Jill.

"That worked when you were a child, darling. It won't work now."

"Leave me alone, Mother, please. I just want to enjoy the pool for a while." She lay back down on the float and closed her eyes. "Alone."

"Desperate times require desperate measures."

Jill laughed. "Sorry, Mother, but I'm not afraid. You just had your hair done; I doubt if you're up for a dip in the pool."

Fool that she was, Jill hadn't counted on her mother's amazing dexterity with the net the poolman used to skim leaves.

"That was a lousy trick," Jill said, slipping into her terry robe and settling down in a chaise longue opposite Agneta.

"You must admit I haven't lost my touch." Her mother poured them each huge, crystal glasses of fresh-squeezed orange juice.

"Your devious ways strike terror in my heart."

Agneta leaned forward and put her hand on Jill's forearm. "The way you've been acting is striking terror in mine, darling."

"The way I've been acting?"

"Darling, you haven't been vertical more than two hours at a stretch since you came home."

"I'm lazy," Jill said, struggling to sound casual.

"What would you say about getting a second opinion of that?"

"I'm perfectly healthy, Mother," she said, her own fears rising to the surface. "I just saw Beauman a few weeks ago."

"Beauman is a gynecologist, not an internist. He doesn't know everything."

"This is a ridiculous conversation." She stood up and steadied herself on the back of her chair. "I'm going inside." *To take a nap.*

Agneta followed her through the patio, the kitchen, the foyer, then upstairs to her bedroom on the third floor.

"Goodbye, Mother," Jill said at the door.

"You look terrible, darling."

"And aren't you glad it's not genetic?"

To her credit, her mother ignored the comment and gently touched the circles beneath Jill's eyes. "You've been losing weight."

Jill sighed as she lay down on her bed, wishing she had the energy to argue with her mother. "You realize you're making me nervous with all this talk, don't you?"

She'd been raised on a steady diet of everything from *Doctor Kildare* to *Marcus Welby*, and if there was anything television medicine had taught her, it was that great love exacted a great price. Romantic heroines on doctor dramas had a hideous incidence of mysterious blood diseases and tragic accidents. It made for wonderful melodrama but for major panic attacks in real life.

"Nervous enough to see the doctor?"

"I'll see Beauman," Jill said. "No one else."

"That's ridiculous. That's not a second opinion."

She held her ground. If she was going to be terrified, at least she'd be terrified by someone she trusted.

"Take it or leave it, Mother. Beauman or no one."

"You win." Agneta sat down on the bed next to her and enveloped her in a cloud of Chanel No 5. "You're probably just anemic. Getting your period again after so long probably shocked your system."

Jill laughed hollowly. "That's an understatement." It had been so long between cycles that she'd all but forgotten what it was like.

"So you'll see Dr. Beauman?"

"Yes," Jill said, unable to hide from it any longer. "I promise."

JILL WAS GLAD that Dr. Beauman had been able to fit her in that afternoon on such short notice. Tony was arriving the next morning, and she wanted all of her crazy fears put to rest so she could enjoy the simple pleasures of being in love.

Well, perhaps the pleasures weren't all that simple, but they were wonderful, and more than anything Jill wanted to be able to stay awake long enough to enjoy them.

So there she was once again, bare-legged and shivering in that terrible little paper gown, in Beauman's examination room.

"I wish you would turn that air conditioner down," she complained as he poked and prodded. "This place feels like an outpost of Siberia."

He palpated her abdomen. "Dieting again, are you?"

"You're changing the subject." She winced as he investigated a particularly sensitive spot.

"You're not here to critique my cooling system, Jillian. You're here to find out why you're so tired."

She looked up at the white stucco ceiling and tried to pretend nothing unusual was happening. *Please, God, don't let there be anything wrong. I'll go to church regularly, I'll contribute to the poor, I'll give up chocolate for the rest of my life, just please let me be all right.*

"Are you dieting?" Beauman repeated.

"No. I just haven't been hungry the last few days."

"Mm-hmm."

She tried to sit up but the nurse gently pushed her down. "What does that 'mm-hmm' mean?"

"How much sleep did you say you've been getting?" Beauman queried.

"Not enough. That's why I'm here."

"If I want one-liners, I'll call Joan Rivers. From you I want answers."

"Fifteen, sixteen hours," she said, looking at her hands. They were mottled and red with goose bumps the size of half-dollars. They were also shaking, but she couldn't blame that on the cold.

"And you're still tired?"

"Yes," she said flatly. "Exhausted."

"Hmm."

She didn't like the sound of that "hmm." In fact, she didn't like much of anything at the moment.

"I'll bet I need B-12." *Why do you look so serious?* "Mother has been telling me that B-12 is the answer to all life's problems." *Come on, Beauman, smile at me or I'll—*

He motioned for the nurse to leave the office, and Jill immediately sat up. Beauman's back was to her as he stripped off his surgical gloves.

"What's the verdict, Doctor?" Her words hung in the air. "Will I live?"

"Oh, yes," he answered, turning to face her. "I'm certain about that."

"No dread diseases? No Rocky Mountain Spotted Fever?"

He shook his head. "As a matter of fact, I'd say you've never been healthier."

Was she going crazy or was a smile cracking through his professional demeanor? Talk about a strange sense of humor....

"Then what is it? I'm not prone to bouts of hypochondria, Dr. B."

He took her hand and held it, cold and shaking, between his two. "Jillian," he said. "You're pregnant."

Chapter Twelve

"Pregnant?" Jill's sharp bark of laughter split the room. "That's ridiculous!"

"Is it?"

Those nights with Tony came back to her in Technicolor detail. "Well, I mean, there's just cause, but we both know I'm sterile."

"Infertile," Beauman pointed out gently. "A very significant difference."

"I don't believe it," she said, her hand resting lightly against her flat belly. "You must be mistaken."

"The urine sample tested positive, Jillian. The blood work will be ready at four." He leaned against the windowsill adjacent to the examining table. "There are certain, incontrovertible changes in your body that spell out pregnancy."

"I didn't think this could happen," she murmured, her body numb. "I didn't think it was possible."

"Frankly, neither did I. But here you are. If my calculations are correct, you'll have a Christmas baby."

She heard the words but they didn't penetrate.

The first time she'd been pregnant, she'd burst into joyous tears in Beauman's office then floated home as giddy and giggly as if she'd polished off a magnum of champagne.

But the first time she'd been young and painfully naïve. When her pregnancy ended with such tragic suddenness, it had never once occurred to her that such things were possible. That they could happen to her.

"I know I should be asking you a thousand questions," she said to the doctor after she dressed and joined him in his office a few minutes later, "but my mind is blank."

"Not surprising, considering the circumstances."

She turned her hands palms up. "Now what?"

"Now you start taking good care of yourself." He outlined a regimen of sleep and exercise and vitamins. "Given your history, I'll want to see you more frequently than usual, but beyond that, no special instructions."

She shivered, pulling her linen blazer close around her body.

"The air conditioning?" he asked.

"Terror. I don't know if I could stand it if anything happened...." She'd rather be sterile the rest of her days than live through a repeat of the ectopic pregnancy that had shattered her dreams.

"Look at me, Jillian. Have I ever lied to you?"

She forced a smile. "Not that I know of."

"There's no reason for me to think you'll have anything but a healthy, uneventful pregnancy and delivery. We're aware of your miscarriage. That doesn't alarm me, but I intend to keep an eye on you. We'll do a sonogram later on if it's warranted." He took off his glasses and rubbed the bridge of his nose. "You'll have your Christmas baby, Jillian. I promise you."

JILL CLAIMED A MILD VIRUS and begged off the family dinner that evening. Instead she had a tray of eggs and toast sent to her room while she tried to make some sense of things.

I should be feeling something. I should be singing for joy. I should be thinking of names and planning a nursery.

Her stomach lurched, and she knew it wasn't morning sickness.

She should be planning how she would tell Tony the impossible had happened. Over and over she heard his words at Grace Benson's house that night. He wasn't cut out for fatherhood . . . he had no idea what real families were all about . . . nannies and prep schools . . . better to leave parenting to people who really wanted it, and he sure as hell wasn't one of that number.

He wasn't a man who courted familial responsibilities. My God, he didn't even want to be saddled with a kitten. She remembered the look on his face when Grace handed her the two calicos.

It was not the look of a man who would welcome an infant into his life.

And who could blame him? She couldn't crawl inside his heart and understand the loneliness he'd suffered as a child. She couldn't know the relationship he had with his father. Not really. Whatever his feelings were on fatherhood, he had a right to them.

Why, if she, a woman who had always wanted a family, was having difficulty accepting the reality of this pregnancy, how was he going to feel?

She didn't want to think about it. She didn't want to do anything but sleep.

She burrowed deeper under the covers and closed her eyes.

Maybe it would all make sense when she awoke.

IT DIDN'T.

The next day, Tony's plane had been delayed at takeoff at JFK, and he'd left a message that he'd grab a car and come directly to the Von Eron's mansion, which was fine with Jill. She was afraid if she'd gone to the airport, she would have jumped on the first plane west and hidden out in Hank's house in Silver Spur until she could come to terms with this unexpected miracle.

She dressed carefully that evening, aware of a numbness that began on the inside and worked its way out. Her movements were slow and deliberate as she pinned her hair atop her head and zipped the slim-fitting black silk dress that obviously wouldn't be of much use to her for the next eight months.

She'd need maternity bras and big cotton gauze shirts and those slacks with the kangaroo stretch pouches in the front and—hell! She couldn't concentrate even on that. None of it seemed real. Her breasts were still small, her stomach still flat. Her thoughts and dreams were still her own private property and not that of the small being growing inside her body.

At the moment she wished it could stay that way.

She tossed down the hairbrush and looked at herself in the mirror.

The fun-loving stranger who'd looked back at her in Nevada was gone. This woman was older, more sophisticated. This woman had huge dark circles under her eyes and hollows in her cheeks and a look of such stark terror that she had to look away.

Be careful what you wish for: You just might get it.

Eight more months of uncertainty.

Eight more months of never knowing if the next day would be the day that that small life slipped away.

But, oh God, how much she wanted this child. . . .

Her hand passed quickly over her abdomen. Poor baby, she thought as she closed the door behind her. Given a mother with a medical history more complicated than the tax law and a father who was likely to say goodbye before he ever said hello.

Not the romantic and wonderful start one might have wished. And here she was about to bring reality crashing down around her.

She walked toward the top of the staircase and paused, her hand barely touching the railing. Peter Duchin's piano mingled with the laughter and clink of glasses. Suddenly she knew she couldn't do it. She couldn't walk down there and make small talk when her entire life had been turned upside down.

She needed time alone, time to hold this miracle close to her heart and make the transition herself.

Curled inside her womb, her child and Tony's was already imprinted with its own set of genes, a combined heritage of the best of both of them. Nothing was going to change that fact.

It was a miracle in a world that held little store in such things.

She hadn't meant to trap Tony in life's oldest web but there it was.

She'd lost her husband because she couldn't get pregnant. Now she'd probably lose the love of her life because she could.

Either the Almighty had a peculiar sense of humor or the fates were even more unfair than she'd first thought.

She found her grandfather in the library smoking a cigar. "When do you go back to the ranch?" she asked without preamble.

He eyed her over his stogie. "In about a month. We're on our way to the Caribbean on Sunday."

"I'd like to use the plane tonight." She told him where she wanted to go but not why and, bless him, he didn't ask.

"You takin' Graham with you?"

"Not this time."

"You two have a fight?"

She shook her head. "Nothing like that."

"He bein' good to you?"

Her hand briefly touched her abdomen. "Very good, Pa." *If creating a miracle is good enough for you.*

"Runnin' away never helps anything, girl. You know that."

"I know that. I just need time to think, Pa, and the ranch has always been the best place."

"All right," he said finally. "It's yours."

She took a deep breath to steady a sudden swell of nausea. "Don't tell anyone where I went."

"I don't like this secrecy, girl." He put a hand under her chin. "You're looking peaked."

"No questions now, Pa, please. You have to trust me on this one."

"What do I tell Graham when he asks where you are?"

She grabbed a piece of paper from the desk top and scribbled a note. "Give him this. Tell him I'm fine, that I just need to think."

Her grandfather looked at her then pocketed the note.

"I'll call Jerry," he said, reaching for the phone as she started breathing again. "The car's out back and the kitchen's empty. You can slip out now."

She hugged him, tears stinging her eyelids. "Thanks," she whispered. "You won't regret this."

"Funny," he said, "but I think I already do."

SEVEN HOURS LATER she was sitting in front of a roaring fire with Hank's dog, Rusty, snoring by her side.

Running away had been easy.

Going back again wouldn't be.

Because when she went back she would have to tell Tony.

And then learn how to live without him after he said goodbye.

"GONE?" TONY ASKED. "What do you mean gone?"

For the first time since he'd known him, Wiley looked uncomfortable. "She says she's gone away to think."

Tony slammed his fist into the hibiscus plant next to him on the patio. "Think about what?"

"Beats me, boy. You're the one with the note."

"The note doesn't say anything."

"Then whatever it is, she ain't talkin'."

"Where'd she go?"

"Now I'm the one who ain't talkin'."

"Listen, Wiley, this is important. Tell me."

The old man took a puff on his cigar. "Sorry. I like you but I like her more. I promised to keep my mouth shut and I'm going to do it."

Tony grabbed the old man by the lapel of his jacket and lifted him off his feet.

"Listen, damn you," he spat through clenched teeth. "I love her. I want to marry her. Where the hell is she?"

When Tony came to, Wiley was leaning over him, holding a bag of ice against the right side of his face.

Tony touched his chin and winced. "What happened? I feel like a palm tree fell on me."

"Sorry, boy," Hank said equably. "I never would've thought you'd have a glass jaw."

Tony sat up on the grass. "You belted me?"

"Had to. No man grabs my lapels and gets away with it."

"Code of the West?" Tony mumbled through his pain.

"Code of the Wileys," Hank said with a grin. "Gotta admit I like your style, though."

"You pack a hell of a wallop for an old man."

"Gray power," he said. "Somethin', ain't it?"

"I'll never look at Social Security benefits in quite the same way."

Wiley sat down on the grass next to him. "You said you love Jilly."

Tony occupied himself with the ice bag.

"Answer me, boy."

"You're not my father, old man."

"Answer me," Hank roared.

"Yes, damn you," Tony roared back. "And she's walked out on me. That make you happy?"

"She love you?"

He rested his head in his hands. "That's what she said."

"So what's the problem?"

"I was hoping you could tell me."

"She needs time to think. Women are like that; they run hotter than Hades one day and colder than a witch's teat the next. You gotta learn to roll with the punches, boy, or your marriage ain't got a chance."

"If you're so damned smart, why have you made so many lousy choices?"

"No lousy choices. Only stupid men. I'm givin' you the benefit of seventy-three years' experience. Take it or leave it."

Things were looking pretty bleak as it was. A little advice from a veteran warrior couldn't hurt.

"Let her be. Jilly has always been a loner. Let her work things out for herself awhile."

"How long is 'awhile'?" The thought of losing her to something he couldn't identify was making Tony crazy. "What if she never comes back?"

"She'll come back. She's always gone away when she had a big decision to make and she's always come back once she made that decision. No reason to think this time'll be any different."

"I'll give her a month," said Tony.

Wiley shot him a look from under his bushy gray brows. "Two weeks."

"And if she hasn't come back yet?"

"Hellfire, boy, you fly out to my ranch and you bring her back kickin' and screamin'. You two are right for each other and there ain't nothin' that should keep you apart."

Tony leaned back and looked up at the stars. "You know, Wiley, you're a brilliant man. I don't know why I didn't realize it before."

Beside him, Hank Wiley lit up a cigar. "You just had to have some sense knocked into you, that's all."

Tony started to laugh then quickly reapplied the ice bag to his jaw. "Wiley?"

Hank took a deep drag then exhaled, the perfect picture of age triumphant. "What?"

"Your cigar stinks."

Hank stubbed out the cigar on the bricks and held out his right hand. "Tony," he said. "Welcome to the family."

SILVER SPUR, NEVADA

AFTER A WEEK AT THE RANCH, Jill began to doubt the wisdom of her actions. Now that she understood the wonderful reason for her constant exhaustion, it bothered her less. She slept when she needed to sleep and, as her appetite returned, began to feel stronger and healthier.

Morning sickness hadn't appeared yet but it was probably right around the corner, so she decided to enjoy the calm before the storm and treat herself to big country breakfasts.

It shouldn't have come as any surprise that she was finding it difficult to fasten her jeans in the morning, and so she took to wearing drawstring sweatpants more often than not.

It was a time of transition, a time to savor the miracles happening inside her body.

And it *was* a miracle. As the realization of her pregnancy took hold, a deep serenity began to take shape, a serenity she hoped would see her through some rough times ahead.

The one thing she didn't like, however, was the loneliness. Strange how she'd never felt lonely at the ranch before. In the old days, it was enough to hear the wind buffeting the house, to have Rusty's graying muzzle resting on her foot, to watch the fire crackling in the grate.

Now, without Tony to share them with, the fun was gone.

She'd come up here to think but she'd done precious little of that.

What was there to think about when you got down to it?

She was pregnant.

She wanted to be pregnant.

Pretty straightforward.

The baby was Tony's.

She loved Tony more than life.

So far, so good.

She told him she was sterile.

It was an honest mistake. Even Beauman had thought it could never happen.

She was five weeks pregnant with Tony's child.

What's the matter, Von Eron? Can't think your way out of this one?

He deserved to be told, and it was time for her to do it.

Maybe it was time to think about going back.

MANHATTAN
The same night

GIVING JILL TWO WEEKS TO HERSELF was turning out to be tougher than Tony would have figured.

Easy for the old man to say "Give her time." Wiley wasn't in love with her. Wiley wasn't looking to spend his life with her. Wiley wasn't staying up all night with his gut twisting inside out wondering what their future would be.

No. Seventy-three-year-old Hank Wiley was off somewhere in the Caribbean with his own woman while Tony lived the life of a monk.

A very celibate, unhappy monk.

He tried movies to pass the time. He tried racquetball. He spent hours working out agendas that could turn Mozart-to-Go into a smashing success.

But what the hell good was Mozart-to-Go if the resident Mozart had taken a powder?

He needed to talk to someone.

On the seventh day of Jill's absence, he found himself standing in the doorway of the library at the Emory Club, watching his father.

The *Wall Street Journal* was neatly folded on the table next to him, a half-empty snifter of brandy atop it. A copy of *Forbes* was open on his lap, but Antony III wasn't reading.

He was asleep.

Funny. Tony couldn't remember ever seeing his father asleep during the day before. He stepped into the room and leaned against the bar.

The blinds at the windows were drawn against the sun—although not much sun found its way to midtown Manhattan. There was just enough, however, to cruelly highlight the gray at the temples, the deep lines around his mouth, the heavy wrinkles surrounding his eyes.

Antony Graham Wellington III was getting old.

Strange that his son had never realized it before.

Watching a man sleep seemed the ultimate invasion of privacy. Tony turned to leave just as his father's eyes opened.

"Tony." He sat up and straightened his tie. "How long have you been standing there?"

"Not long," Tony said, sitting opposite him. "Didn't mean to wake you."

"I was just resting my eyes," the elder Wellington said. "I didn't know you were back in town."

"I wasn't supposed to be."

"Problem?"

"I wish I knew."

Both men fell silent. This was the point where most of their conversations died—unless they escalated into an argument, which was a whole other story.

Maybe it was because Tony had been living on the edge of his emotions for days now, but there was no way he could stop this time even if he wanted to.

And this time he didn't want to.

"Feel like going to dinner?" he asked.

"I'd like that a great deal, Son."

The word struck a chord too deep to be ignored. He met his father's eyes. "That's the second time you've called me that, Dad."

His father held his gaze. "Do you mind?"

Hell. It had been the strangest week of his life. He might as well go for broke. "No, I don't mind at all." He took a deep breath. "But I didn't think you knew you had one."

Wellington shook his head, and Tony saw himself thirty years from now, growing older, growing lonely, growing scared.

"Forget I said it, Dad. Bad choice of words."

"Maybe not," his father said. "Maybe there are a few things that need to be said."

"Listen, I—"

His father raised his hand to silence him. "You're the best thing that ever happened to me, Son. Without you, my life would have been empty." He looked away. "Empty."

Tony swallowed hard, caught up in more conflicting emotions than he could have named.

Wellington stood up and patted him on the shoulder. "Come on," he said. "We have a lot to talk about."

Tony stood up and embraced his father for the first time.

"Yes," he said. "Twenty-eight years to be exact."

SO MANY THINGS he'd never known.

So many things he'd never bothered to ask, never cared to explore, never tried to understand.

Tony and his father sat together over drinks, over dinner, over dessert, learning about the many ways they'd hurt each other—and the many ways possible to heal.

His father's grief when Tony's mother died had been a huge bird trapped inside his chest, clawing its way through his heart. The small boy, so like his mother, had been a bittersweet reminder of loss, and Antony had not known how to deal with any of it.

Business was the one thing he could count on, the one unchanging thing in a world unstable and terrifying.

"I wanted to provide for you," he said to his son over coffee. "I wanted you to be as secure and safe as it was possible for a child to be." His hand shook as he lit a cigarette. "My own life was so devoid of love that it didn't occur to me that there was any other way to be. Don't make that mistake, Son. Don't turn away from love."

He thought about Jill and the future that stretched before them, an unfurling of shiny gold ribbon. "I couldn't turn away if I wanted to. It's gone too far for that."

His father smiled at him, and in his eyes Tony saw two decades of estrangement begin to crumble—one brick at a time.

"And us," Antony said, resting his hand atop his son's. "Is it too late to take another chance?"

"No." Tony's voice was strong and sure. "I don't think it's too late at all."

And so it began.

SILVER SPRING, NEVADA
Three days later

THERE WAS SOMETHING to be said for the past.

Jill stretched out in the huge, old, claw-foot tub in the master bath and let the gardenia-scented bubbles rise over her breasts and throat. How wonderful that Pa had been his stubborn old self and decreed that even though the plumbing was being modernized, he was drawing the line at the claw-foot tub. "They don't make 'em like this anymore," he had said, and Jill had to agree.

Taking a bath was the most interesting thing to happen to her all day.

It was the most interesting thing to happen all week. Up until today, taking a shower had been number one.

What a miserable day it had been.

First, morning sickness decided to make a guest appearance, followed quickly by a dismal, drenching rain that showed no sign of letting up. The storm made a shambles of television reception and, thanks to a fallen tree, she couldn't even use the phone to call for service.

And, to top it off, solitude wasn't half as invigorating as it used to be. Now she wished she'd been smart enough to make sure she had a car. At least then she could make a getaway. She used to relish these long, luxurious times spent alone at the ranch.

Falling in love with Tony Graham Wellington had put an end to that. She thought about him all day, and he invaded her dreams every night. It had even gotten to the point where she thought she heard him calling to her.

She tilted her head to one side and listened. Nothing. Not even Rusty's snoring.

"Get a grip on yourself, Von Eron," she muttered, letting some more warm water into the tub. "You're being ridiculous."

This was just another example of what love had done to her: turned her into a lonely, pregnant woman who took lots of bubble baths and talked to herself. At least when Rusty was in the room she could claim she was talking to the dog.

She turned off the water with her foot and settled back.

There it was again—a low male voice coming from the other room.

Impossible. If anyone were at the door, Rusty would be barking his head off. All of the help were gone for the day, and she was certain she'd locked all of the doors.

But damned if it didn't sound like Tony's voice.

"That's it," she said, standing up and reaching for a bath sheet to wrap around her body. If she didn't go out to check, she'd be waiting there like Janet Leigh in *Psycho* but without the shower curtain.

She flung open the bathroom door and screamed.

Tony was sitting on the end of the couch not twenty feet away, scratching Rusty's belly.

"Glad to see you, too," he said.

She pulled the towel more closely around her body. "What in hell are you doing here?"

He stood up and approached her. "I could ask you the same question."

"I left you a note. Didn't Pa give it to you?"

He pulled a piece of cream-colored stationery from his jacket pocket. "He gave it to me." Slowly he began to rip it into confetti. "Can't say I think too much of it."

Her heart was pounding so loud she could barely think. "I told you in the note. I need time to be alone." *Damn you, Tony. This wasn't the way I had it planned.*

"You've had time."

"I said I would be gone a month."

"Sorry. You'll have to settle for two weeks."

"You could have called. You scared the hell out of me."

He motioned toward the phone. "Out of order. I tried from the airport."

"You could have waited."

"The hell I could." He closed the space between them, and she quickly maneuvered herself to the other side of the desk. "We have a few things to settle."

You don't know the half of it.

"I'm going to kill Pa for telling you where I am."

"Don't blame Hank. I would've figured it out sooner or later."

"How did you find the ranch? Your sense of direction isn't the greatest."

"I hired a small plane. That monogram of trees is a dead giveaway." He grinned as she readjusted the towel. "Did I interrupt something?"

"My bath."

"Don't let me stop you."

Damn that sexy, wonderful smile of his. "If you'll excuse me, I'm going to get dressed."

She headed for the bedroom down the hall.

"Don't follow me," she said over her shoulder. "I want my privacy."

He ignored her. "You've had all the privacy you're going to get. I'm not leaving until we talk."

"We'll talk *after* I get dressed."

"We'll talk *while* you get dressed. Face it, Jill. You're stuck with me. Besides," he said, somehow managing to put a good-natured leer in his voice, "it's not like I haven't seen you naked before."

"Oh, go to hell," she mumbled, fighting down a ridiculously inappropriate smile.

She forgot about morning sickness and the rain and the fact that she'd missed three nights of *Mr. Ed* reruns. For the first time in weeks she felt wonderfully, totally alive.

The man had the most unusual effect on her.

She strode into the bedroom and flung open the door to the cedar closet while Tony stretched out on her bed. "Make yourself comfortable, why don't you?"

"Thanks," he said, flipping through the *People* magazine resting by her pillow. "Do you think Princess Caroline's marriage will last?"

Jill pulled out a pair of sweatpants and a baggy, denim shirt. If he was going to surprise her, he was going to get what he deserved. "Frankly, my dear, I don't give a damn."

"What about Hank and Mary? Do you think their marriage will last?"

She glanced at him over her shoulder. "Are you running a survey?"

He leaned back against the pillows. "In a way. When you're about to ask the woman you love to marry you, it helps to know how she feels on the subject."

She closed her eyes and leaned against the door of the closet, clutching both the towel and her sweatpants. "Don't," she whispered. "Not yet."

"Look at me, Jill."

"We have to talk."

"I love you."

"Tony, listen to me. There's something—"

"I love you and I want to—"

"Shut up," she said.

His eyes widened. "What?"

"I said shut up. Don't talk. Don't move. Don't do anything. Just hear me out."

He folded his arms across his chest and waited.

"I didn't plan this. I didn't expect this. I know it's not what you bargained on."

"You're not making sense."

"Be quiet!" Her voice shook alarmingly, and she feared she would start to cry. She'd been so damnably teary the past few weeks that nothing would surprise her. "I only found out the day before the engagement party. I could hardly believe it."

He threw his legs over the side of the bed and started walking toward her. "Is there someone else?"

She pulled the towel up over her breasts. The sweatpants and shirt fell unnoticed to the wood floor. "You're making this very difficult, Tony."

"Good, because this isn't exactly a bed of roses for me, Wiley. I came here to ask you to marry me, not break up."

"Let me finish."

He grabbed her by the shoulders. "Is there someone else?"

She hesitated.

"Damn it, Jill! If there's someone else, tell me."

She started to laugh, a high, almost hysterical laugh that took both of them by surprise. "Well, in a way there *is* someone else." He let go of her immediately and backed away toward the window. "Tony, wait! You haven't heard it all."

"I've heard enough," he said. "You wanted space; I should have given it to you. I'm out of here."

She moved in front of him, blocking his way out the door. "Tony," she said, letting the towel slither down to her feet. "I'm pregnant."

THERE WAS SOMETHING about a beautiful woman without her clothes on that made it hard for a man to think straight. Maybe it was the sudden rush of blood away from the brain or a drastic shifting of focus. Whatever it was, he found it impossible to hear over the wind-tunnel rush of a thousand pounding pulses going wild.

"What was that?"

She moved away from him. "I said, I'm pregnant." Her hands lightly grazed her breasts then her belly. "I think I'm beginning to show."

He sat down on the edge of the bed. "I must be going crazy. I thought you said you couldn't—"

"That's what I thought, too." She gathered up the towel and wrapped it around her body once again.

He took a few deep breaths in an attempt to get some needed oxygen to his brain. "When? How?" *Pregnant. She's pregnant.*

"My best guess is that night at Fire Creek."

"Grace's house."

She sat down next to him on the bed, and he felt dizzy from the scent of gardenias blossoming around her. "Yes." Her voice was soft. "Maybe it *was* the blueberry pie."

"I still don't understand."

She sighed and drew one bare foot lightly over the polished wood floor. Her toenails were painted a delicate pink and they reminded him of perfect, iridescent opals.

He must be going crazy.

"I don't understand, Tony. My doctor doesn't understand. But there you have it. I'm pregnant anyway." She turned and smiled. He couldn't remember ever seeing a more beautiful sight. "The baby's due Christmas Day."

And that's when it happened. A laugh started from some hidden part of him, a place buried since childhood and ignored all these years. The place in his heart that understood what was innately mysterious: the connection between parent and child, that deep abiding love that defied the odds.

He'd found it again with his own father, and now the woman he loved was giving him the chance to discover it with their child.

She jumped to her feet.

"I'm glad you find it amusing," she said, her voice high and tight. "I'm not asking anything of you, Tony. I want you to understand that this is nobody's baby but mine."

"Say that again."

A flicker of concern passed across her face. "I said, this is nobody's baby but mine. If you want visitation rights, you're welcome to them but I—"

"Why would I need visitation rights?"

She nodded and moved toward the door. "Right. Why would you need visitation rights? Forget I said anything."

She started for the kitchen, the darkened ends of her blond hair, wet from her bath, spilling across her slender shoulders. He reached her before she made it to the end of the hall.

"I'll repeat: Why would I need visitation rights if we're married?"

She stared at him, those huge gray eyes of hers as beautiful now as they'd been the first time he saw them.

"You don't know what you're getting yourself into," she said. "It's everything you don't want."

"You don't know what you're getting yourself into, either," he said. "Why should you be the only one?" He dropped down on one knee before her. "Marry me," he said dramatically. "Marry me and make an honest man of me."

"You're a fool," she said, but a smile began to light up her eyes. "An absolute idiot."

"Maybe," he conceded, "but I still intend to marry you."

This was what he'd been looking for all his life, the thing that gave meaning to all that came before.

"Don't propose to me out of some outdated sense of honor," she said fiercely.

"Don't give me credit for honor," he shot back. "I proposed to you before you said you were pregnant."

She ignored him. "This is a different world. I can manage on my own."

"*I* can't," he said, taking her hand. "There's no way in hell I can manage without you."

She was weakening; he could feel it in the way she held his hand. "What about those loose ends you had to tie up?"

"No more loose ends," he said quietly. "I've burned my bridges, cut my ties, wiped the damned slate clean once and for all. No more looking around the corner to see what's coming next. It's you, Jill, now and always. I don't know how to make it any plainer than that."

"That's pretty plain." She hesitated. "You hate being tied down. Remember what you said to Grace about responsibility and parenthood and—"

"I'm evolving," he said. "It happens to all of us, sooner or later."

"Oh, Tony," she whispered. "I don't want us to make any mistakes."

"Come with me." He led her to the study on the other side of the house with Rusty trotting right behind them. "You're forcing me to pull out the heavy artillery."

"Fair warning: I can't be swayed by diamond rings," she said.

"No diamond rings."

"Fancy cars don't do it for me."

"You're in no danger."

He made her close her eyes then led her into the room and sat her down on the sofa.

"Okay," he said after a minute. "My last-ditch attempt."

She opened her eyes and started to cry.

The two calico kittens she'd fallen in love with at Grace's tumbled all over her lap, vying for her attention.

"I can't believe this!"

"Believe it," he said. "You should see what they did to the inside of the car."

"You did this for me?"

He laughed nervously. "I sure didn't do it for me, boss lady." He sat on the arm of the sofa. "Well," he said, "what do you say, Jill?"

She stood up and put the kittens back into their box then looked over at him. "You do know what this means, don't you?"

He stared at her blankly.

"I'm pregnant. You're going to have to change the litter box for the next eight months."

"We'll hire somebody," he said, continuing to stare at her. "Top dollar."

"My doctor is in Palm Beach, but I don't want to live there after the baby is born."

"Great. I don't want to live in New York."

"We could buy Grace Benson's house. She said it was for sale."

He pulled a legal document out of his pocket. "Beat you to it, boss lady. I signed the papers this afternoon."

"I always did like your style, Tony IV."

"Does that mean yes?"

"No," she whispered in his ear. "This means yes."

And then she kissed him, and he finally understood what magic was all about.

Epilogue

FIRE CREEK, NEVADA
Two years later

If there were any joy greater than sitting under a tree with his great-grandson, Teddy, asleep on his lap, Hank Wiley didn't want to know about it.

Oh, he'd had himself some good times back in the old days, but those old memories were nothing compared to what he was feeling today.

"Surprise parties," he'd mumbled to Mary as they pulled into the driveway of Jill and Tony's huge ranch house. "Waste of time."

His wife poked him in the ribs. "I'm warning you, Wiley," she'd said in that fierce way of hers. "Those kids have been planning this for weeks. Everyone flew out to be here, including Tony's father and his lady friend, and so help me, if you ruin it for them, I'll never forgive you."

Well, he hadn't ruined it for them, not by a long shot. He laughed and joked. He ate the chow and drank the booze and had himself a high old time but, the first second he could, he grabbed Teddy and made off for the tree on the hill.

The view of the mountains was breathtaking. Blue lupine and brilliant red snowdrops covered the sides in a blanket of color. Evergreen white-barked pine. Mountain hemlocks and red fir. Nature in all her unbounded glory, free of the hand of man. He prayed the land would still be that way when this beloved child grew to manhood.

He held the sleeping boy close to his heart. *Wake up soon, Teddy,* he thought. *There's so much to show you before I go....*

So much to pass on to the next generation and beyond. Another hundred years wouldn't be long enough to teach his great-grandson all he needed to know. This hilltop alone had a thousand stories to tell.

And, of course, the hilltop was where they found him.

The pride in him ran fierce as he watched his Jill and Tony make their way up the hill toward them. She wore a flower-sprigged pink dress. The skirt lifted and billowed in the wind, and she laughed up at her husband, her beautiful face glowing in the way it had since that first day in Las Vegas. Graham had changed into a pair of rugged jeans and shirt and looked as if he'd been born to the Western life. The look he gave Jilly made Hank turn away and smile.

Some things, after all, were private.

Jill had turned into a real fine woman, and Graham—he never could get used to thinking of him as a Wellington—was a match for her, every inch of the way. In fact, he was good enough to be a Wiley, although Hank had never told him. People with numbers after their names could be real touchy about things like that.

He liked to think he was responsible for their marriage and, in a way, for little Teddy, but the business—well, Mozart-to-Go was all theirs. Graham was one hell of an entrepreneur, and within months they had a network of musicians out touring the country.

And, each summer, Jill and Tony—and Teddy now, as well—hit the road themselves, crisscrossing the mountains of northern Nevada and the plains of Kansas, going places their privileged lives had never allowed them to go before.

They'd created a real fine life for themselves and given life to the child who slept in his arms.

Knowing that everything he believed in lived on in his granddaughter and her husband and child was the best damn birthday present any man had ever been given.

And to think his challenge to Jill that long-ago night on the beach at Palm had started it all....

They sat down on the grass next to him as Teddy smiled in his sleep.

"Wore him out, did you, Pa?" Jill gently brushed a lock of pale gold hair off the baby's forehead.

"Sure did," he said, his voice husky. "He's some boy."

"He's part Wiley," Graham said fondly. "That counts for something."

Hank looked at them both.

"This was some shindig," he said, clearing his throat. "I want to thank you for doin' it. Took the sting out of turnin' seventy-five."

Jill gave her husband a wifely look. "You see? I told you he didn't know."

But Graham was his kind of man and he knew better. "Tell her, Pa," he said. "Tell her you weren't surprised."

Hank thought about the way families tended to build themselves, not just from bone and blood, but from intangibles like love and friendship and honor—all the things that made life the wonder that it was—and he smiled at them, the children of his heart.

"No, Jilly," he said at last. "I wasn't surprised at all."

Family: The secret of life.

He'd make sure to tell Teddy all about it when he was old enough to understand.